FLASH

BY MICHAEL CADNUM

MICHAEL CADNUM

FLASH

Farrar Straus Giroux
New York

For Sherina

Even the slip
of a moon
draws the sea

www.fsgteen.com

Library of Congress Cataloging-in-Publication Data
Cadnum, Michael.
    Flash / Michael Cadnum.— 1st ed.
        p.   cm.
    Summary: Relates one momentous day in the lives of five young people
in the San Francisco Bay Area, including two teenaged bank robbers, a witness,
and a wounded military policeman just back from Iraq.
    ISBN: 978-0-374-39911-5
    [1. Robbers and outlaws—Fiction.   2. San Francisco Bay Area (Calif.)—
Fiction.]   I. Title.

PZ7.C11724Fl 2010
[Fic]—dc22

2009014145

FLASH

1

"When will you show them the gun?" asked Milton. He and his brother were sitting in lawn chairs in back of the house.

The morning clouds were burning off, and the sunlight was bright beyond the shadow of the house. San Francisco Bay Area summers were usually like this—half hot, half cold—and the East Bay was enjoying a characteristically dry season.

"Let me hear you say it," Milton insisted.

Sometimes he wanted to hit Bruce over the head. Bruce would take a good deal of hitting—he had a large, round head with close-cropped hair and he smiled a lot. The smile did not mean that he was happy. It meant he was stronger than most people, and that he intended to take advantage of it.

Milton Borchard was eighteen and had graduated from Albany High School earlier that summer. Bruce was sixteen and had dropped out of the same school. Milton found his younger brother to be a lot of responsibility, and sometimes he wished he could think of a way of getting rid of him.

At last Bruce complied and said, "I'll show her the gun after this."

He took a paper out of his inner pocket and displayed the note, which had been folded and refolded until it was limp, the large words in red Magic Marker. THIS IS A ROBBERY. He folded it again and put the paper back inside his leather sport coat, stylish and good-looking, except for the dark stain along the left cuff.

"Don't take the first bag of money they give you," Milton cautioned.

Bruce nodded. He was trying to be patient, and even gave Milton one of his smiles, looking every inch the sort of person who got things done.

Bruce had worked a few nonunion construction jobs until earlier in the summer, when the local developer ran out of funds, and you could still see the line of pale skin on his forehead where the hard hat had kept off the sun. He had dropped out of school to make money. He had failed.

Just then Mom was in the doorway, trying to hear what they were talking about. Her bathrobe had her name stitched across the left breast: LOUELLA. As though her sons might mistake the baggy, worn garment for one of their own.

Milton lifted his finger and Bruce kept his mouth shut.

Mom looked and listened, and you could see her wondering what the hell her two boys were about to get into. Milton tried out his own smile: *Just the two of us talking*.

Mom shuffled back into the darkness of the interior, a big woman looking even bigger in pink terry cloth. She did jigsaw puzzles of famous artworks in her spare time, which she didn't have much of. She worked with a committee trying to win increased pensions for sugar refinery employees and their families.

Louella Borchard had emphysema and swollen feet, but she had worked as a dispatcher for the Port of Oakland for twenty years. She had the demeanor and mental habits of a person who was accustomed to ordering forklifts to berth ninety-eight and making sure they got there. One of Milton's first memories of his mother was her cursing at a cable TV installation crew for stepping on her geraniums, and the men in white hard hats apologizing, scared of her.

From then on, Milton had the impression that his mother would not hesitate to tear the head off anyone who crossed her. Just like Bruce.

Mom had survived on her own in recent years. Her own mother had drowned in the Russian River during a flood, when Milton was five years old. Her father had been killed in Sparks, Nevada, in a fight with someone trying to break into his car. Milton thought that luck had long ago abandoned his mother, and he felt sorry for her.

She was in bad health, and she needed cash. Milton was determined to see that she would get it.

"Just don't take the first bag of money they give you,"

Milton repeated, hating himself for nagging his brother, but someone had to make the plans. He had the feeling that if you could read Bruce's mind you would sense a hot current of self-assurance accompanied by nothing. No thoughts, no inner dialogue—just white-hot nothing.

"Because they'll sneak a dye bomb into it and the cash will blow up on us," Milton continued, "and we'll be two dyed clowns with a bunch of useless money."

The bank would open at nine-thirty, and Milton calculated that the bank employees might take a few minutes to get their cashboxes full of currency, nice rows of twenties and fifties. It was ten minutes after nine now.

In maybe half an hour he and Bruce would be bank robbers.

2

Nina Atwood woke suddenly.

She had been in a deep slumber after hours of wakefulness, worrying about the unusual challenge awaiting her in the forthcoming day. But now she was wide awake in an instant.

There was someone in the house.

She knew this—but how? Had she heard a sound?

The predawn was dark. The digital alarm clock and the points of light on her laptop all gave off enough ghostly glow for her to see the hulk of the desk chair and the backpack hanging from the bedpost.

These homely objects appeared alien now, awkwardly sinister. She sensed the quiet of the big house beyond her open bedroom door and the all-but-silent chuff of wind over the eaves, the midsummer clouds sifting in off San Francisco Bay.

And then she heard a definite, undeniable something—a sound, no question. The hardwood floor creaked, and the carpet whispered under a footstep. The muted noises probed her sense of security, and she felt outrage.

This trespasser, whoever he was, had just turned on the floor lamp in the living room. The lamp was too far away to illuminate her room, where she grasped the blankets, pulling them around her body, but she sensed a pale quasi-light that insinuated into the space.

Her father had warned her to lock the house up, and of course she had, but this was probably an expert, one of those people who can break a lock by breathing on it, and now she was in trouble.

Frighteners, they were called, thugs who crept into a house and scared a man's family, or worse than scared them. If you owed money, these were the guys who made sure you paid it.

She held the quilt up to her chin. She was scared. She wondered where she had left her cell phone, and reckoned that it was in the bottom of her backpack, or in some other inconvenient place where it would be impossible to retrieve the thing silently.

The entire town of Albany had been in turmoil lately. There had been a drive-by shooting barely half a mile away right before the Fourth of July, with a man working on his car fatally wounded. And someone walking his dog had found a dead body on Albany Hill just last week, an unidentified male, the cause of death still under investigation.

The small Bay Area town, wedged in between Berkeley to the south, with its university and politics, and Richmond to the north, with its refineries and decayed apartment warrens, was no longer a peaceful place to live.

She was alone in the house and the only solid plan she could come up with was stymied—her brother's nine-millimeter Beretta was locked in the safe in his old bedroom closet, kept secure while he was on duty in the military. She had thought she might need the gun someday, and she had figured out the safe's combination and made sure the pistol was loaded, but there was no way she could get her hands on the gun now without making a lot of noise.

She was helpless.

She held her breath and let it out slowly, keeping very still. Whoever it was, he was being quiet, too. Nina heard the cushions of the sofa give off an almost imperceptible sigh.

And then she heard the Hello Kitty key chain make its characteristic jingle.

SHE HAD TO BE SURE, because if she was right, something wonderful was happening.

Too wonderful to believe.

No one but her immediate family knew about the key secreted under the potted agave plant at the end of the porch. Her brother had bought the key chain himself, and stuck it there under the big terra-cotta urn.

The key chain made a further racket, tossed into the large ashtray no one ever used except for extra quarters and keys, just the sort of thing her brother always did, sitting down when he first came home.

But Carraway was in a military hospital in Germany, recovering from almost being killed.

Wasn't he?

She spent a breathless moment before the mirror, her reflection blurry as she put on a bathrobe, her new haircut every which way—four o'clock in the morning and no time to make herself look human.

She ran down the hall, her bare feet padding quickly down the cold hardwood.

Then she hesitated.

Despite certainty that this had to be her brother, she had a growing sense that he was still too badly injured. The army chaplain on the phone had mentioned sepsis and intravenous antibiotics.

"A nasty piece of ordnance zigged through Carraway's insides," was the way Sergeant Palmer, one of Carraway's army buddies, had described the injury in a phone call.

The television was on, something in Cantonese, then an ad for stain remover, and finally CNN.

She said her brother's name.

She called it again, louder.

3

So much depended on Bruce.

Milton had wasted a lot of energy keeping the guy out of trouble. The robbery scheme had been more than a much-needed moneymaking strategy—it was a way of directing Bruce's energies.

For instance, Bruce had a habit of picking fights with passing motorists. It wasn't road rage, it was pedestrian rage. Everyone knew drivers speeded, they double-parked. But Bruce took it personally. This was not a good idea, given the string of drive-by shootings all over the Bay Area recently. Drivers these days were armed with Glocks and hollow-points, and an aggressive pedestrian had been shot dead in San Francisco earlier that summer.

But personal safety was not an issue with Bruce. He had bloodied a guy's nose outside the Albany Theatre three months before, a driver who nudged his car into the cross-walk while Bruce was walking in it. He had picked the guy up out of his little blue Alfa convertible, and if Milton had not been there to pull Bruce off the stunned, scared driver, they would have had serious difficulty with the law.

Bruce had been suspended from high school twice for fighting, but had never been arrested. Milton felt that you had to admire Bruce, but on the other hand, you didn't.

He felt that strange, unhappy stirring inside again, a jealous feeling not at all friendly toward his brother. Like maybe hearing that his brother had been put into jail would not be such bad news. This was the way he had felt since he saw his brother with Billyana Venova, putting his arm around her on Solano Avenue, Billyana responding by leaning her head against Bruce and walking along like the two of them were stuck together.

Billyana's family was from Bulgaria, and her father taught comparative lit at San Francisco State. She spoke with a sultry voice and had an exotic accent, a full figure, and long sable hair. Her father had forbidden Billyana to spend time with Bruce, and so their intimacy had been a secret, even from Milton. Seeing them together had been a very unpleasant surprise.

Milton had spent the Memorial Day weekend in Santa Rita County Jail, waiting to be arraigned for being drunk in public. He had been drinking red vermouth you could buy from Jay Vee Liquors on Central Avenue, where the cool-eyed counter clerks watched for shoplifters and drug deals over by the porn and the Snickers bars.

Maybe he had been drinking to keep from feeling jealous toward Bruce, but such hard romantic disappointment was new to Milton, and he did not know why he had felt trapped in such bitterness. He had passed out on the sidewalk in front of the bowling alley on San Pablo Avenue, and the cops of Albany, California, did not want the town to turn into another one of those troubled San Francisco Bay Area communities, with people stretched out on the ground, unconscious, nowhere to go. "It's a little early in the day for a nap," Officer Dean had said, tucking Milton into a cage car and locking him up for the long holiday weekend.

The trial was yet to be scheduled, but the court-appointed attorney was a breezy man named Paul Casper who said Milton could plead guilty and ease into community service, picking up trash along the shoreline during one of the Save the Bay days held every summer.

Milton was accustomed to being exposed to the learning of his elders, and not only state-licensed teachers. He had shared a crowded cell with a grizzled, alcoholic bank robber named Arnold Reese, who had explained all the drawbacks to a life of crime, by way of encouraging Milton to reform and not take up robbery for a living.

Milton had listened carefully, but drew a different conclusion from the one the veteran felon had suggested. Milton had heard on the news that one out of every hundred Californians was in a correctional facility, and he was surprised at how many incompetent criminals there were.

"That blown-up money will be the evidence that puts your butt in the joint," said the professional criminal. His warning only made Milton ambitious to pull off a bank job cleanly.

He had begun looking at pictures of celebrated felons on the Internet, everyone from Billy the Kid to the shadowy, muffled figures caught by bank security cameras, and felt that there was a brotherhood of criminals out there, and that most of them were less intelligent than Milton.

Now Bruce climbed out of the lawn chair and gave a meaningful look at his Nike multifunction wristwatch. He slipped the pistol out from the interior of the jacket. He stood at an angle so Mom couldn't see.

If there was one sour detail in the crime Milton had planned, the gun was it.

"Are you sure we shouldn't look around for a better gun?" asked Bruce, holding the pistol down low with one foot forward, a classic stance that made him look unquestionably dangerous.

Milton suspected there was a gun or two in the Atwood house, down the block, with the big brother in Iraq getting half killed, the father always off somewhere, and cute little Nina all alone. And Major Wanstead, with his perfectly manicured front lawn, was always putting a gun case into the trunk of his Chrysler—surely the retired soldier must have a handgun hidden away in his nightstand.

Milton admired the way Bruce looked with the pistol and the leather jacket. Milton wished he had half his younger brother's good looks, but where Bruce was tall, blond, and broad-shouldered, Milton was mouse-brown and lean.

Milton said, "Tuck it in your belt," hoping to God his brother wouldn't get into a gunfight.

4

How thin he looked!

This was her brother, definitely, the same Carraway she had always known and loved.

But he was different. Even with only one lamp turned on she could see that her brother was as handsome as ever, but gaunt. His face was expressionless, his body tense. He turned off the TV and stepped toward her, one arm out, not the usual two-armed hug her family employed, a family of long, rib-cracking embraces.

"Hey, Nina," he said quietly, putting his sinewy arm around her.

She hesitated, afraid that she might cause harm by touching him. The surgeon on the phone had said that it was a miracle Carraway was alive.

"Carraway, I thought you were in the hospital." In Germany, she could not add. What was he doing here?

He smiled. "Not anymore."

His short, dark hair was tousled, and he was unshaved,

dressed in scruffy civilian clothes, an outsized white T-shirt and lumpy gray cargo pants. A denim jacket lay tossed over the armchair. He did not look at all like a national guardsman who had just been promoted from specialist to sergeant.

She wiped her tears of happiness. Carraway was customarily terse and straightforward, a no-tears guy, but he was blinking tears, too, and she was happier at that moment than she had ever been in her life.

He did hug with both arms then, emotion and family custom taking over, but he clasped her gently, a man with something wrong with him even after three months of medicine.

"Dad's not home?" he asked, releasing her.

"He's in Milan," she said. "He left in a hurry and he might not be back until next week."

She meant to communicate in those few words a world of trouble for her father, and she knew that if Carraway was anything like his old self he would guess. Milan and London were where the exporters lived, the people who had to be convinced to let Dad's payments continue to slide.

Carraway got the point. He gave his *Say no more* nod as he looked around the living room.

"He sold the old clock?" he asked, sounding surprised.

"He got a good price."

Carraway took a few steps into the entrance of the dining room. He had his former loose stride, she noted, and carried himself with only the trace of a limp. "No butter dish," he exclaimed. "And the box of silverware is gone."

Carraway stopped at a blank space on the wall, where the photo of General MacArthur had held pride of place for many years, the famous picture of the general returning to the shores of the Philippines in World War II, signed by the photographer, Carl Mydans.

"He found a buyer on eBay for big money," she said.

Actually, he had been disappointed in the closing price—but he had not had much choice. The future had changed for Nina, too. With weeks to go before she began her senior year, she had put aside all thoughts of college. She expected to help her father's business when she graduated.

She had not discussed this with him—but that was her plan, and he would have little choice but to accept her help. Mr. Wu, her counselor at Albany High, had given her a list of possible scholarships, but she wanted to see her father's prospects improve before she gave a thought to her own future.

Her brother shook his head in disbelief, putting his hand flat on the wall where the photograph had hung. "Dad loved that picture!"

Carraway was right, but for the moment she was not interested in material possessions. There was something she needed to know, and she had to come right out and ask. "Does your wound hurt?"

She meant the question earnestly, solicitously. When

their mother had been alive, it had been her nature to inquire.

But Nina was also ardently curious. What was it like to be nearly killed in an explosion?

She wasn't tremendously surprised when Carraway responded by pulling up his T-shirt and revealing his healed incision. Carraway had an aggressively matter-of-fact approach to things that amounted to a sense of humor.

Nevertheless, the scar was a shock, a long vertical wound that ran down her brother's torso. She felt her own front, reflexively, realizing the distress of such an injury, and the permanent aftereffects.

So easy, she thought. It was so easy to die. And so easy to randomly, accidentally not die.

She felt shaken, instantly let in on one of life's cold secrets.

He let the shirt fall back into place, and gave her a smile—ironic, but proud, too. "The doctors said it's a tribute to battlefield medicine."

That, she thought, and Carraway's stubborn, quiet hold on life. She asked, "Did it hurt?"

"No," he said, "It never did hurt that much."

"There had to be some pain," she said. She was fully prepared not to believe him. Carraway didn't like an emotional fuss, especially when he was the cause.

"Even when I swelled up and my blood pressure dropped to almost zero," he said smoothly, no emotion in his voice, "pain was not the main issue."

"What was the main issue?"

Carraway sat down at the dining room table, the big walnut tabletop reflecting him in the bad light. "The issue was not caring," he said. "As I was being flown out of Safwan Airfield I didn't care whether I lived or died."

This upset Nina, and she could not query him further. She could not imagine her brother not wanting to live.

"I didn't want to die," he said gently, as though prompted by the need to reassure his sister. "But I was so weak, so absolutely drained of strength, that I could not scrape together enough energy to care one way or another."

Nina considered this solemn confession. Her ailing mother had seemed that defenseless toward the end, the ovarian tumor erasing her will.

Carraway picked up her photo, the one they kept in a koa-wood frame in the middle of the table. Nina had taken the picture herself at the age of ten. The image showed a woman with sandy blond hair and a smile, an outdoorsy person in a sun-yellow blouse with mother-of-pearl buttons. Nina still had the blouse, hanging in her own closet.

There are things that only you can do.

This had been her mother's credo. Her mother had worked as a translator, specializing in technical European prose, turning French essays on lead glazes and Portuguese commentaries on optics into English. She had given Nina her first camera, but the absorbing nature of Mom's work had made her seem distant—friendly but not quite present, even when she was. She was always reaching for a dictionary, or scribbling a reminder on a Post-it, saying that Dad was late again.

"How much trouble is Dad in now?" asked Carraway, setting the photo carefully back where it belonged. He asked with the same tone he had used the time she broke the teapot with the Wiffle bat, ready to help her surreptitiously glue it together. He lifted one hand, a lightly impatient gesture, guessing what she was about to say.

"I know it's what Dad calls a cash-flow crisis," he said. He gave the phrase an ironic emphasis. With Dad, car trouble was a transportation shortfall, and a messy bedroom was an example of delayed maintenance. "How bad?"

"The dollar is weak against the euro, and the rent on the Solano Avenue shop is up forty percent." She did the books for her father's import business. He dealt in Belgian chocolates and Italian wines and other gourmet products, and she had seen the problem get worse, month by month. "He's broke."

Worse than broke. He was in serious, dangerous debt. But she didn't want to talk about their financial challenges right now.

She wanted to hear more about Iraq. For the last year and a half, ever since he had enlisted in the California Army National Guard, Carraway's e-mail had been briskly enigmatic, beyond any brevity military censorship could possibly require.

Even his messages from the medical center in Landstuhl, Germany, where she had expected that relief at being alive, and pain medication, would have eased him into a little more communication, had been scant. He had sent out *Every day, in every way*, or some such mock-serious e-mail. She and her dad had been reassured, because the mantra "Every day and in every way I'm getting better" had been a family joke, expressing the sort of brittle optimism her family had always made fun of. She had taken his snappy complaints about delays in getting his medical transfer as a sign that he was going to be in good health again some day. But the doubts had remained. Now she wanted to hear about combat, and how it happened that he was still blessedly alive.

She asked if he still liked his coffee black. They were out of milk. She busied herself with brewing a pot, her hands trembling with the excitement. She kept looking back to make sure he had not vanished.

"What made the doctors decide to let you go?" she asked, getting two mugs down from the cupboard.

"They didn't."

She didn't like his answer. Something about this new version of her brother made her uneasy.

5

Milton was worried about the gun.

If Bruce was forced to use the firearm, he couldn't. What appeared to be a classic, army-issue forty-five was in fact a cigarette lighter.

The facsimile was cunning, and had the details and heft of the actual firearm. You could rack the slide and set the safety. But when you pulled the replica's trigger a little flame appeared at the end of the barrel, and the flame stayed on until you pulled the trigger again. It was some novelty manufacturer's idea of a coffee table joke—have a few drinks and light your Marlboro with a pistol. Milton had traded a pair of Pentax binoculars for the thing, and now he saw the danger of carrying around a weapon that looked authentic, but wasn't.

Bruce was toying with the thing, the tiny flame flicker-ing and pallid in the morning sun. Milton felt a stab of affection for his brother, a sensation of keen protectiveness. If a police officer fired real bullets at Bruce, one of the reasons would be that fake pistol.

Bruce stuck the phony weapon into the top of his Lucky Brand denims. Then he checked the side pocket where the black garbage bag was peeking out just a little, folded tightly, with more than enough capacity to hold the thirty or forty thousand dollars in mixed bills Milton was anticipating.

Bruce buttoned the jacket, size fifty and a good fit. The seller at the flea market had said the stain was cranberry juice, but Bruce called the garment his dead-guy jacket, convinced that the previous owner had been stabbed. He liked that—a coat with a vivid backstory.

The brothers both went out into the far reaches of the rambling backyard, behind the garage.

THE BLACKBERRIES AND POISON OAK of Albany Hill grew over the property line, a fence that sagged and wandered.

The hill was a land-bound island, seventy-five yards high at the north crest and more than a quarter-mile long, a sloping, wide-flung geological upwelling, bristling with eucalyptus trees. The hill was home to thriving bird life, snakes, and, in past seasons, the occasional drug dealer. Beyond the hill to the west was Interstate Eighty and San Francisco Bay.

Milton could smell a trace of char in the morning sunlight. A blaze had started up along the south slope of the hill just two weeks previously, and Albany's sixteen-man fire department had needed trucks from Berkeley and El Cerrito to stifle the flames. Only a small portion of the hill had burned, but the urban wildland was all kindling this time of year, dry star thistle and rye weeds waiting to flame up.

Bruce was busy now, tugging the tarp off a stolen Ford Taurus four-door—the getaway vehicle.

The car was ten years old, sage-green, 120 on the odometer, and dented on the right passenger's side. Bruce finished pulling off the plastic cover and took a step back, admiring his temporary possession.

The Borchards owned a little-driven, rust-pocked Toyota pickup and a Ford Econoline van. The van was an impound, bought at an auction in the police auto yard in Oakland when Dad was still alive. The van could carry everything, from truck axles to beehives, but driving the family vehicle to commit a robbery in broad daylight was out of the question.

The entire backyard was a collection of abandoned hopes and enterprises. The fiberglass hull was evidence of their father's plan to sail to Hawaii, and the Cessna wing frame was part of a scheme for the father and his sons to get their pilot's licenses, once Dad put together more of the airplane.

An explosion at the sugar processing plant in Crockett had taken Peter Borchard's life just five years before. He had been an assistant security chief, meaning that he kept the post orders on file and filled in when the replacement shift was late, which was often.

The medical examiner said Peter Borchard had been legally drunk at the time the storage tank blew its lid, which meant that the security company offered one third the usual settlement, and the Borchards took it. For the family, their father had grown over the years of his absence into a legendary character, a man who had left behind fragmentary monuments to his enthusiasms.

One of those enthusiasms was car theft. The car Milton stole had to be a Ford because he had found a diagram on hot-wiring the Ford steering column in one of his dad's old notebooks. Stealing a car had taken a long time. As easy as it looked, he still had to find a vehicle someone had forgotten to lock up. That effort had required long walks up and down the streets of El Cerrito and Berkeley at night, trying doors and attempting at the same time to be hard to see.

The plan was to escape with the money in a car that could not be traced to them in any way, and to abandon the automobile. Then the two of them would return home through the system of creeks and flood-control drains that coursed down through the residential neighborhoods from the hills toward the bay.

The scheme had merit. Coyotes and deer used the drainpipes to find their way in secret down through the busy neighborhoods, where the deer helped themselves to flowering plants and the bounty of pear trees, and the coyotes were rumored to nab the occasional kitten or puppy. But the plan was a challenge, too. Neither brother had ever actually tried it before.

"We better get going," prompted Bruce, the morning sun in his hair.

Milton understood at that moment that his desire to send his brother into the bank was not simply an expedient part of the plan. He wished, in a recessive, badly understood corner of his soul, that his brother might go into the bank and never come out.

Now that the car was exposed, Bruce was subtly in charge, or at the very least Milton sensed their partnership becoming more equal. Milton was the planning guy, but Bruce was responsible for the action.

Milton gave a nod and his brother hunched down inside the Ford. Bruce fiddled with wires in the steering column, and the engine coughed and started, idling raggedly. Bruce sat behind the steering wheel and worked the accelerator, getting the engine rhythm to smooth out.

Then he got out of the car, leaving the engine running, an unsteady rattling noise under the hood.

Bruce put on his mask, experimentally—a San Francisco Giants knit watch cap that had been cut with scissors so he could pull it all the way down and have openings for his eyes. He looked like trouble.

Milton put on his disguise, a pair of Maui Jim sunglasses he had bought for a few dollars—they were held together

27

with a paper clip, one wire of the clip fitting into the hinge where the screw was missing. He donned an Oakland A's baseball cap, the bill pulled low. He tugged his shirt out so it looked sloppy and shapeless. Milton knew from his study of security camera images that these adjustments rendered him all but impossible to identify.

"You look good to go," said Bruce, pushing the watch cap up so his face was bare once more.

Milton got in behind the steering wheel and set and released the parking brake a few times while Bruce got into the passenger side.

6

The stolen automobile contained small details of another person's life: a pocket pack of Kleenex, an empty bottle of Dole apple juice. Someone had left a turquoise-blue hair band on the backseat and a booklet of coupons for bleach and hair conditioner, with a page torn out.

Milton was troubled by these particulars. He got the impression that a woman, single and hardworking, had owned this car. She still owned it, if you looked at the facts clearly. He did not like the thought of her waking, wondering where her favorite blue hair band was, and then peering out at the eerily empty parking place beyond her front lawn on Key Route Boulevard.

Milton felt protective toward women, including his own mother. Mom spent hours on the computer, participating in a chat room composed of aggrieved former employees of the sugar refinery and their families. Once a month she attended meetings in Crockett with a pro bono attorney, hearing how someday a big class-action settlement would descend on them like a rain of cash.

Milton thought: Maybe, maybe not.

Milton and Bruce both took a long moment to buckle their seat belts. Milton knew this was not an ironic waste of effort. Being stopped by a traffic cop for the infraction of not wearing a seat belt would devastate their plans, and besides, Bruce took traffic violations very seriously.

But it was a meticulous step in what was turning out to be a very anxious morning, and Milton felt the day lose color as he backed the Ford down the driveway, not driving very straight, running over the geranium bush beside the driveway, the entire garden shabby and neglected.

"We'll return the car," said Milton, not believing it for a second, "back where we stole it from, when we're done."

Bruce did not bother responding.

The neighborhood was tidy and modest, well-kept little lawns and metal awnings. Each small house was on a diminutive parcel of land, as though the town had been designed for petite folk, with careful habits. The Borchard house, at the end of the street beside the wild fennel and blackberry of the creek, was the single eyesore.

"Whatever you do," said Bruce, "don't kill the engine."

His voice was tense, but the tension was a source of strength. Bruce was more courageous than his brother—Milton could see that.

"Coming toward us," said Bruce, matter-of-fact. "A police car."

The black-and-white cruiser was headed in their direction, and with cars parked along both sides of the narrow street, there was not room for both of them to pass.

They were about to have an unavoidable collision with law enforcement.

7

Nina put the empty coffee mugs down on the table.

"You're not AWOL?" she asked.

"No, I'm not," Carraway said. "Not exactly."

In civilian life, he had collected rents and delivered documents for Mr. Leblanc, a businessman who brokered mortgages and bought foreclosed properties. One of the reasons Carraway had enlisted in the military was because providing security to Mr. Leblanc had gotten Carraway to thinking about a career in law enforcement. The National Guard had a successful military police program at Camp Roberts, in the sun-drenched, oak-studded hills of California's coastal range. Training at Camp Roberts would be perfect preparation for a career fighting crime.

Nina had always thought that Carraway would make a good cop.

"Why did you sneak into the house?" she asked.

Carraway gave her one of his deadpan glances. "Why not?"

"You scared me."

"I'm sorry, Nina. I had to have a few minutes to myself. I wasn't ready to talk to Dad, for one thing. You know how he is."

She certainly did. Dad talked nonstop, he chattered, he paced. Everything made him nervous—good news, bad news. Dad was a life-consuming, needful force, and he made everyone tired, particularly the people who loved him.

"I have trouble picturing what happened," she said. "I mean, how you got hurt. I got different descriptions, depending on who I listened to."

He flicked his gaze at her. "Who have you been talking to?"

"The chaplain, of course, and the doctor. And that friend of yours, Sergeant Palmer. He sent a few messages about your condition, encouraging us."

"He's not my friend," said Carraway, a seething, quietly determined sound to his voice. "Not anymore."

"I thought," said Nina, "that you and he went on patrol together."

"We did," said Carraway.

"What's wrong?" she had to ask.

She wanted to add that Sergeant Palmer sounded like a very friendly individual. He had an enjoyable range-rider accent, a cowboy drawl. "Carraway doesn't complain," he had told her on the phone. "That's his way of complaining." And yet there had been something about Palmer's phone manner that had seemed slightly off-key, a hint of possible trouble.

"I can't prove anything," said Carraway, "but I am afraid Palmer used some very bad judgment just a few hours before I almost got killed."

"You mean, he did something to put you in danger?"

"No," said Carraway. "That's not what I mean."

This was unusually enigmatic, even for Carraway, so she persisted. "What did Jerry do?"

Carraway considered his answer.

"He was escorting a couple of detainees back to the refugee camp," he said at last. "And I think something bad happened."

"Like what?"

Carraway kept his voice flat, but she could hear his emotion. "The guys he was escorting never arrived."

"You mean—"

"Shut up about Jerry, OK?"

He had never sounded so harsh before.

This wasn't just a new, worn-out remnant of her brother. This was a stranger, tough-minded and secretive. He scared her.

Maybe, she thought, Carraway had done bad things, too, and didn't want to talk about them.

Carraway realized that he had troubled her, and he changed his tone to one of friendly inquiry when he asked, "Are you still seeing Terrence?"

"All the time," she said, giving the words some spin,

meaning: Don't say anything unpleasant about my boy-friend.

He got the point, and gave her an acknowledging smile. "You know I've always liked him."

Anyone would, she thought.

She had known Terrence since her family moved from Oakland when she was eight years old—Albany was celebrated for its safe and capable schools, while used hypodermic needles and spent nine-millimeter shells were often discovered at her former playground. She enjoyed the hours she spent with Terrence, and he had encouraged her to meet with the gallery on College Avenue—the main source of her anxiety in recent days.

"Terrence doesn't believe in war," said Nina.

"What does Terrence believe in?" Carraway inquired, a little cocky, but genuine, too, really wanting to know.

Terrence believed in patience, and attention to detail. He believed in her. But she felt that the subject of Terrence, even his name, was special, and belonged in a context apart from armament and injuries. The coffeemaker made a noise like someone being strangled, the way it always sounded.

She changed the subject.

"The National Guard," she said, "will probably give you a medical discharge. Won't they?"

He gave her one of his looks, friendly but not friendly at the same time.

"I mean," she continued, "if you want out of the military."

"I'm on medical leave right now," he said. "Technically I'm assigned to a rehabilitation center in Oakland. Except I'm not, really. The private first class handling my case let me fill out the paperwork myself, and I left a lot of blanks. I could go to Kauai and claim that I was just following orders. My being here talking to you is perfectly all right."

"You mean, your superior officers don't care where you are?"

"No, for the time being, they don't."

She had thought the military was better at dealing with people than this. In her mind, the military was a lot like the post office, but it did not deliver mail. It delivered tanks, bombs, medics. She found her brother's attitude toward the armed forces flippant and even potentially sinister.

When she had heard that just before the near-fatal explosion Carraway had been trying to rescue the occupants of an American tank, she had been proud but unsurprised. She had always known that her brother was capable of heroism—as a girl she had seen him calm a rottweiler in its death throes, reassuring the animal with his soft voice.

But she also knew that her brother liked getting into a fight. She had seen him step up to fellow athletes on the softball diamond and the soccer field, and more than once he had been benched not so much for violence—he could contain his temper—as for his threatening manner. With the death of their mother, six years before, Carraway had ceased to be a boy. Overnight the teenage Carraway began to talk the way he did now, scary-quiet.

He had become emotionally cooler after Mom was gone, but Nina had sensed a new authority in him. He could do good, or he could do bad. She liked this about him, although this characteristic was often unsettling.

"The TV news," she said, "said that you might get a Bronze Star."

"And a Combat Section Badge," he said, sounding unimpressed, "and a Global War on Terrorism Medal, not to mention a Purple Heart."

"Tell me what happened."

He shrugged, but this was not a shrug of indifference. She understood: it was hard to talk about.

She wondered if she would ever be able to understand this newly different version of her brother—even more moody and tense than before.

Maybe even dangerous.

8

Nina changed the subject again, back to something safe. She asked, "What do you want for breakfast?"

"What do you have?"

She opened the refrigerator. They did not have much. "Do you still not eat eggs?"

There were two of them in the refrigerator, hardly a feast.

Their father kept samples of his import business in the kitchen—balsamic vinegar from northern Italy, and pure cocoa from Holland, but none of the delicious foreign goods added up to a meal. Pictures of Dad decorated the kitchen: Theodore Atwood getting the Chamber of Commerce Merchant of the Year certificate, shaking the governor's hand. Dad was a handsome man with a dark mustache and a warm smile.

But she had seen this beaming expression alter over the years, as his business expanded and, at the same time, made less money. In recent pictures his trademark grin was more of a grimace, like a man staring into a very bright light.

"Eggs are fine," Carraway was saying. "They don't bother me anymore."

Carraway was twenty-one, but he had an older person's regard for a careful regimen. He had forsworn butter and whole milk in high school, and sugar, too, in his personal war against a rich diet.

Nina thought that perhaps Carraway's antagonism to eggs had been a little bit of an anti-Dad policy. Dad loved eggs, and described himself in interviews—meaning it to sound funny—as an egg man.

"I have discovered," Carraway said, a trace of humor in his voice, "that eggs and cholesterol aren't life's major problems."

She had never known the coffeemaker to be so slow. It finally finished the job, and then the beverage spilled out of the mugs because her hands were shaking. She would have thought that her happiness at her brother's return would feel more peaceful than this.

"What is life's major problem?" she asked.

"Money is the biggest problem," he said. "For everyone. Maybe some toast would be great."

But she knew how his conversations usually went. He changed the subject, and then he changed it back. She made no move to leave the table, leaning over its polished surface so she could see her reflection in the early morning light. There were three slices of whole wheat bread in the bread box, not enough for a real breakfast.

"Are you going back to work for Leblanc?"

"He promised me he would take me back," he said. "He also assured me that if I needed any help he would always be there."

"And you believed him?" she asked, keeping her voice level, the way her brother did, flat and full of meaning.

"I did."

"What if he doesn't give you your old job?"

"He has money," said Carraway. "I'll ask for a loan."

"Dad can't afford any more debt."

"Are you still taking those spooky, beautiful pictures of freeway underpasses?" he inquired. "Maybe you can sell some of those, make some money, and get famous."

The question made her happy. "You won't believe it. I actually have an appointment with the Gilliam Gallery on College Avenue this afternoon."

"Congratulations, Neeno," he said, breaking out her old nickname.

She was moved by the sound of her pet name, and she couldn't speak for a moment, she so deeply appreciated her brother's praise.

She was apprehensive about the interview with the gallery owner, not sure that she was ready to have her photographs on public display. An artist friend of her father's had arranged the meeting, and there was no guarantee that Hank Gilliam would like her photos. Terrence had told her it was a slam dunk—but Nina was not so sure.

"An article on the Web," she said, "described the gallery owner as 'acerbic, opinionated, and cunning.' "

Her brother lifted his eyebrows in mock-horror. "All three?"

She laughed. "That's what it said."

"If he doesn't agree to display your pictures," he said, "I'll cut his legs off."

She gave a weak laugh, but the remark worried her.

"My Beretta is still locked up in the safe, isn't it?" he asked.

"The gun is loaded and waiting," she said. "You don't really need it, though, right?"

Carraway had a license to carry a concealed weapon—Mr. Leblanc had arranged it with the Alameda County sheriff. Nina had formerly found the pistol he had worn holstered on his hip to be fascinating and even sexy, in a secret-agent sort of way, but dangerous and not a part of the world she inhabited.

Lately, however, she had begun to see the weapon as a possible necessity. The once sleepily calm town was treacherous now. Nina's favorite Korean restaurant had suffered a takeover robbery the month before, and two customers had been pistol-whipped.

"I didn't leave it loaded," he said.

She didn't want to make him mad, but he might as well know. "I cracked the safe."

He put his fingers around the mug and seemed to enjoy the feel of the heat. "You didn't really."

"No, not exactly, but I found the combination, and it works."

He gave her a guarded look, admiring and cautious. "You found the combination how?"

"I know the way you think."

CARRAWAY SAID that he had to see the backyard.

The dawn was casting shadows, but a thin overcast covered the sky, and morning was an idea, not yet a fact.

Nina wondered how he felt, putting his hand out to touch the pear tree, with its branches held up high, the pears still green.

Their mother had been alive and healthy when they first moved to this house, and she had dug up the aged apple tree in the back garden with the rest of the family, a major project. The old tree had been stubborn, gnarled, and capable of presenting only a few blossoms in the spring when the family had first arrived, and even fewer small red Spartan apples as the summer wore on.

After shovels and a pickax had been applied, a rented chain saw had been necessary, Dad protected by oversized goggles, yellow sawdust everywhere. This pear tree was the replacement, and shortly after it had been put into the ground Mom had begun seeing specialists. She had read books on using mental imagery to combat illness, took large tablets of codeine, then Vicodin, and at last pearls of morphine from an eyedropper.

"The tree hasn't grown that much!" Carraway said. "I thought it would be like this." He raised his arms, and for a few moments Nina could see her brother as he had been while Mom was alive, like the time he had been excited that a raccoon had taken a piece of smoked salmon right from his hand.

"The deer haven't paid a visit this summer," said Nina. "Except once. Dad scared them off with an air horn."

She didn't know how the animals wended their way from one garden to the next, over the tall, bougainvillea-covered fences, but they did—youthful bucks and cautious, brazen does, beautiful and annoying, claiming what was not theirs. Or they used to. In an attempt to frighten off the deer, their father had bought an air horn, a red cylinder like a fire extinguisher, that loosed a terrible blast of noise. A trespassing deer had hurried off at the first blast, and no other deer had dared visit since.

"Does the bowling alley still serve breakfast?" Carraway asked.

He seemed to be changing the subject again, but Nina knew better. Carraway changed topics without really switching, a way of buying time to think.

"The Royal Cafe has better hash browns," she said.

"Let me take a shower, and get into some of my street clothes," he said. "And then we'll go to breakfast and I'll tell you what it's like to get blown up."

9

The supposed police car Milton and Bruce were encountering was indeed a black-and-white Police Interceptor Crown Victoria. However, there was only a faint scabby disk where the municipal emblem had been scraped off, and the words WATCH COMMANDER were faint scars on the left rear fender.

Milton pulled to one side and let the car ease by on the narrow street.

Many East Bay police departments were on such tight budgetary restrictions that they had auctioned off some of their rolling stock, and reduced the hours of cops on the street. The Albany police were no exception, reducing front office and cutting the payroll. This was one of the reasons Milton felt so optimistic about today's venture—the cops were ill-equipped and understaffed.

The driver of this former squad car was a guy with a shaved head and aviator glasses, a match for the ones Milton was wearing, except no paper clip was holding the frame. He had a dragon tattoo over his ear—blue scales, with pink flames coming out of the creature's mouth.

He was definitely not a cop.

Bruce and Milton laughed, glad to release some tension.

Then there were only a few neighbors to go by unobserved. The major was bent over, out by the sidewalk, clipping his lawn with an electric edger. He did not seem to notice them. Jocelyn Hurlow, the cutie from Bed Bath & Beyond, didn't notice them either, getting a hurried, late start on her day, piling into her Honda Civic.

And there were cats—the neighborhood teemed with cats of every variety, calicos to Siamese, surly to friendly. Milton could not see the cats, but he knew they were there, watching. Milton had a grim thought: If he ran over one of those sinuous, fleeting animals, it would not only delay his day, with regretful exclamations all around. The accident would also be a very bad omen, to put it mildly.

Milton drove with exaggerated care, coming to a full stop, signaling, and letting the car roll down toward San Pablo Avenue well under the speed limit. He was grateful to see that the stoplight was red. He was perfectly satisfied to put off what was going to happen.

But the light changed quickly to green and Milton gave the car a little more gas as he made the right turn with all the fragile caution of a student driver, pulling into the center of the avenue, letting oncoming cars go by, and then making the left turn.

The immediate parking place he wanted, right beside the East Bay Bank, was taken by a red BMW, but farther along was a parking space by the curb almost as good.

Milton put the gearshift in neutral, the automatic transmission making subtle mechanical alterations somewhere in the workings of the car.

He was about to set the parking brake, but Bruce said, "Just let it idle."

"I don't like the way the engine sounds," said Milton. The vehicle clattered, fit for a junkyard.

"One of the cylinders misfires," agreed Bruce.

"No wonder she left the car unlocked," Milton responded.

He was making conversation in the nervous, anything-to-keep-talking way people do when they are tense, and when Bruce opened the passenger door Milton wanted to keep right on chattering.

But he didn't. The smell of the outdoors washed over Milton, sun on the sidewalk and salt air from the bay. A bird chirped and a car started up somewhere. Too bad, thought Milton, you can't push *pause* and have life freeze into stillness.

But Bruce was already gone, not saying *See you* or giving his older brother a nod, letting the passenger door swing shut without latching, a detail Milton had not planned.

———

THE WAIT WAS LONGER than Milton had anticipated.

He kept the engine running, putting his foot on the accelerator every few seconds to get the RPMs up. The fuel gauge showed a quarter tank of gas, more than enough, unless they got involved in a chase on the freeway.

The rearview mirror displayed the corner of the bank, San Pablo Avenue with its light morning traffic, the red BMW sitting there unoccupied, a beer truck across the street with a big bottle of Miller Genuine Draft emblazoned across the side. Milton reached up with his gloved hand to adjust the mirror, and then quickly put his hand back down out of sight, aware how ominous it must appear, a ghost hand.

Then an unexpected and cumbersome conveyance made its appearance.

A big, boxlike battleship-gray vehicle made the turn off San Pablo Avenue and rolled past Milton's Ford—a Loomis armored car. The driver slowed down, as though considering double-parking, trapping the Borchard car against the curb. That would be a disaster, Milton thought with alarm.

He rolled down the window, and then rolled it right up again, not wanting the armored car to wedge him in against the curb, but not wanting to get into a memorable conversation with an armed guard, either.

The armored car rumbled forward, and made a turn into the bank parking area, but as the large security vehicle disappeared from Milton's view he had the bare beginnings of a new idea. It was just the briefest, sketchiest sense of a fresh strategy, but Milton did not have time to shape this possibility because someone was rounding the corner in the rearview mirror, hurrying away from the bank, and nearly falling down.

10

Terrence Quinion always held his breath at this point in the eye exam, and Dr. Saltz always told him it was OK to breathe.

He did it now, backing away into the darkness with his insistent, precise point of light.

"It's OK, Terrence," he said with a chuckle. "Go right ahead and breathe."

The doctor leaned in close again, and Terrence's vision was lit up by a vista of his own inner eye, red veins searching like rivers and capillaries reaching out into the vitreous outer regions. The radiance shifted as the opthalmologist's attention swung from one district of the retina to another.

Terrence had been visiting Dr. Saltz's San Francisco office for years, and he was always intrigued by this part of the examination, the part where the unexplored world was his own body.

Terrence sensed something new about the doctor this time, an upbeat intensity in the man's posture.

"You have a healthy pair of eyes," said Dr. Saltz, snapping on the desk lamp.

"Except I can't see very well."

"Except for that," agreed Dr. Saltz.

He was writing something, the rollerball pen making emphatic, quiet sounds on stiff paper. "Your acuity is abridged, but otherwise you have what I would call exemplary eyes."

Terrence couldn't drive, and he had to watch movies within an arm's length of the video screen. But he could perceive colors perfectly well, blue being his favorite. Every shade of green also gave him special pleasure. He could see movement, too, and if someone stood near—someone like Nina—he could look right into her eyes, his close-up vision perfect.

He and Nina shared an interest in making the ordinary world fascinating. In Terrence's case that meant capturing the twitter and response of birds with his digital recorder. And for Nina it meant taking twilight photos of bus stops and parking garages, and using her skill with color to make them come alive.

To Terrence without his glasses, Dr. Saltz was a pastel rumor, a watercolor that had been immersed in water and left to flower into indistinction.

"You can keep wearing the same prescription," said Dr. Saltz.

This surprised Terrence. Every six months he paid the doctor a visit, and nearly every six months he had needed new glasses.

Dr. Saltz handed back the glasses with Armani frames and Terrence put them on. Even wearing glasses, his eyes were 20/180, which meant that he was almost legally blind. At twenty feet away from an object he could see what normal eyesight could perceive at one hundred and eighty feet away.

"This is an important development," said Dr. Saltz.

Terrence liked Dr. Saltz, but he associated the man and his office with doubt, and a growing knowledge that as he got older he was closer to being completely visually handicapped. Not that he was expected to become lights-out blind. But his severe congenital myopia was on its way to making him less and less reliant on what his eyes could see.

"Remember when we talked about surgery?" asked the doctor.

Surgery was not a concept that Terrence could contemplate without a sensation of inner turmoil. He associated surgery with TV shows featuring patients going into convulsions. Nina's brother, Carraway, had undergone field surgery in Iraq, and Terrence had been uneasy over his apparent prognosis, his intestine perforated by a chunk of shrapnel.

As harrowing as surgery sounded in any event, the thought of eye surgery in particular made Terrence recoil.

When an ER physician at Kaiser Hospital had to take a blackberry thorn out of his mother's eye, Terrence had not been able to stay in the same little examination room, but had wandered up and down the hall, praying for the ordeal to be over.

The prospect of surgery on his own eyeballs made Terrence feel the stirrings of severe uneasiness. The thought was intolerable.

And yet there was another side to the prospect.

Terrence kept his voice steady. "You said laser surgery was a challenge in my case."

"I said it was not advisable, because your cornea is probably too thin. But I also said there were other options."

Terrence recognized a degree of revisionism in the doctor's recollection. He had said that Terrence and his mother would have to wait until Terrence was finished growing. Then, with Terrence fully adult, they could explore the possibility of surgical correction. The science was still developing, Terrence knew, but along with uneasiness he felt undeniable hope.

"Tell me," said Terrence, "what you mean."

11

We'd be considering a number of possibilities," said the doctor.

"Like what?"

"Well, like maybe lens implants—permanent contact lenses, you might call them. The optical technology is always advancing. How much surgery can improve your vision is an open question, over time, even if the initial improvement is modest. You've begun to stop growing, so we can start to think ahead."

"You mean my pituitary gland has finished its job?" Terrence asked.

"You seem to be slowing down," said Dr. Saltz, "but at seventeen you still better wait for another couple of years. I grew an entire inch taller when I was nineteen."

Terrence was a little amused at the thought of Dr. Saltz growing taller, because the man was noticeably short. Dr. Saltz was a puckish, gray-haired individual with a small dark beard. His office was decorated with antique maps, continents Terrence could not observe without stepping right up to them, but which he knew were intriguing pizza-shaped territories, how the world looked before anyone knew how it really looked.

"But I think," said the doctor, "that we should begin to investigate further opportunities." He said this emphatically, but with an openhanded gesture that Terrence could make out as a wordless *Why not?*

Dr. Saltz had a knee brace on his right knee, a contraption Terrence could not see very well, but which he understood to be a device that let the doctor walk around. The doctor was old enough to be anybody's grandfather, but he climbed cliffs in Yosemite, and fell off them, too.

Despite Terrence's anxiety and his relief that the surgery was still a year or two in the future, he was happily teased by the prospect of having something akin to normal vision. He felt joy at the thought—real, pure-gold joy. Normal vision was certainly worth the anxiety and discomfort of surgery—no question.

But Terrence was wise to the way the world worked. If you grew too confident, you were vulnerable to almost certain disappointment.

"We can't afford expensive surgery," Terrence said. "We have health insurance through Kaiser. My appointments with you are out of my mom's pocket and some months—"

He didn't complete the thought. Annette Quinion ran

an estate liquidation service. Her ex-husband, Terrence's adoptive father, had a newly pregnant wife, and there were some months when there was very little income.

"I want you to see Dr. Peavey out in Orinda," the doctor said, writing a note on a sheet of paper. "You should go soon, so he can start planning."

Terrence felt his mouth go dry.

"Dr. Peavey is the best in the profession," Dr. Saltz said, perhaps realizing that Terrence was unhappy.

Terrence had understood that Dr. Saltz could do the surgery himself, and this had offered great comfort. The thought of seeing a strange physician in an unfamiliar office made Terrence anxious all over again.

"When am I going to hear your sound effects?" asked Dr. Saltz, in a cheerful effort to change the subject.

Terrence was glad Dr. Saltz had asked.

"I'm trying to capture the sound of a red-tailed hawk hunting call," said Terrence.

"They have a particular hunting call?" asked the doctor.

"Birds are always making announcements," said Terrence, surprised that even a smart, nature-loving man like Dr. Saltz did not study birds more closely. "Even when they just say *Here I am*."

Terrence recorded bird sounds for Lucasfilm. His mother had arranged an estate sale for someone who worked for the Marin County movie producer. Terrence had e-mailed some of his samples by way of audition, and they had offered him a contract. Whenever a movie needed a raven or a California quail, instead of using stock bird sounds they'd contact Terrence for something fresh.

At least, that was the plan. The money involved had been small, so far. But when Dr. Saltz added now, "I bet you could make a career as a sound technician," Terrence was pleased.

That, he thought, was his hope.

THE WALK FROM Dr. Saltz's Post Street office to the Bay Area Rapid Transit station was always an adventure, because the sidewalk was crowded and Terrence had to keep to the shadow so the morning sun would not diminish what little visual acuity he had.

He was used to the route, however, and even felt a degree of personal pride in his ability to maneuver past flower stalls and people pushing dollies of cardboard boxes into lobby entrances.

Terrence had been adopted at birth, and did not know who his biological father and mother might be. The dad he grew up with now lived in Iowa with his new and pregnant wife, testing cures for corn blight for the U.S. Department of Agriculture and wondering if he could raise twins on a government paycheck. He and Annette had divorced a couple of years before, but Terrence kept in touch by e-mail, getting news of tornadoes in the next county, or floods wiping out the soybeans.

There was a little aloofness between Terrence and his

father, a touch of coolness, but Terrence felt untroubled. He did wonder sometimes where his genetic forebears might be, and whether his unknown blood relations had undergone corrective surgery, or if they peered around at events through thick lenses.

His transition eyeglasses got dark when he stepped out into the sun, and Terrence knew that in the flowing sunlight of the street, with the little bit of muscle he had put on doing push-ups and sit-ups, he was not bad-looking. He must be the descendant of centuries of fairly attractive men and women who had learned to think better than they could see.

On the BART platform, Terrence stayed well away from the rubberized yellow strip that marked the safety of the waiting area from the danger of the tracks. A man had committed suicide here the week before, and if there was anything that troubled Terrence more than the thought of eye surgery, it was the thought of getting tangled in the wheels of an onrushing train.

He stayed well back, even when the train had wheezed past, and had safely stopped, and people had begun hurrying in and out of the open doors.

Terrence was careful—you never knew what might happen.

12

Before they left for breakfast, Nina called their father—it was late afternoon at the Hotel dell'Orso in Milan, and Dad's appointments for the day would have been completed.

At the beginning of the phone call, before he heard the news, Dad sounded weary and resigned, but he made every effort to disguise his mood from his daughter. He was changing his shirt, he reported, getting ready for dinner with a creditor from Verona, and she let Dad babble on, pleased to have a secret he did not know.

Dad loved to talk. He chattered to himself in the shower, and he talked to strangers on BART. He talked in his sleep, and over breakfast he recounted dreams in which he had talked his way out of trouble. He won friends easily with his rapid-fire chatter, his vigorous interest in where people lived, shopped, and ate lunch. Old friends, however, kept their distance. He had worn them out with his nonstop monologues.

"Guess what?" she said when she could get a word in, interrupting his story of cabdrivers, the honest ones versus the dishonest.

" 'Guess what?' " her father echoed, sounding suddenly wary. "You want me to guess? What, for example. Give me a hint."

She could make out the sounds of a bed creaking as he sat, sure there was bad news.

"It's not bad news," she said.

"What is it?"

It was a joy to tell him. The truth was, she loved hearing him talk, even when he drove her crazy. She realized how much she did not enjoy listening to some of the other people she knew.

Like Myrna Hearn, for example, their next-door neighbor, a fountain of opinions, wondering why she didn't take more pictures of roses. Or babies. *Everybody thinks kittens are precious.*

Dad was deeply moved and excited to hear that Carraway was back home. But, having lived on a diet of bad news recently, he had trouble entirely believing it.

"Is that even possible?" he asked. "Home? In California?"

"He's here," she reassured him. "As big as life."

"How does he look?" her father asked, and when she said that he looked good she felt that she was not exaggerating, exactly. But she was tweaking the truth a little, using a little verbal Photoshop.

He was speechless for a long moment, and she thought she could hear the far-off voices of Italian passersby, down in the street below the hotel.

At last he managed to say, "That's wonderful!"

Wonderful was probably his favorite word, and when an event really was wonderful his voice went up in pitch. *Wunn-derful*.

"Wonderful," he had repeated, his voice a falsetto whisper.

Carraway came out of the bathroom then, his hair sticking up wet from the shower, and stood in the living room holding the cell phone to his ear saying that he felt great, and adding that one way or another he was going to take care of Dad's problems.

MYRNA HEARN was watering her lawn in a mauve flak jacket, military fashion having penetrated the just-in racks at Smile Styles on Solano Avenue. Her hair was the color Nina associated with cat food, brown and glistening.

Myrna yoo-hooed when she saw Carraway and waved water in his direction, a dazzling spiral in the sunlight.

"Welcome home, handsome," she called.

Myrna was tall, and when she talked, barking dogs shut up. Myrna was the go-to person Nina was supposed to call, day or night, with any trouble. Dad thought the world of Myrna. Nina was impressed with her, but did not like her. She ran an investment firm on College Avenue, but the right rear taillight of her silver BMW 328i was fastened on with duct tape. Nina's sense was that, these days, even people with money didn't have it.

Carraway said hi, taking his time, not minding the woman's attention at all. Carraway liked people, in his quiet way, and he liked women especially—older, younger, he didn't mind. Nina tugged his arm, hurrying him away.

"I think she suffers from ought-ism," Nina confided to her brother as they walked down Washington Avenue. "She likes to tell everyone what they ought to do. She says she really hates to tell me this, but no one likes photos of buildings. *Why don't you take nice pictures like you used to?*"

She scared herself a little, sounding for a few seconds just like Myrna. She felt momentarily commanding. She used to be afraid that her dad might take up a romantic relationship with Myrna, but as yet there had been no sign of anything but neighborly friendliness between them. Someday, she suspected, her father would begin a relationship with a woman, and she did not look forward to the possibility.

Was it wrong, she wondered, to want to keep her father for Carraway and herself, the three of them separate and secure?

Rick Cotteral, the chiropractor, was up early, taking his pug for a walk, a plastic bag of dog droppings in his hand. He lifted the bundle in greeting from across the street, and called to Carraway that it was good to see him. His office on Solano Avenue displayed a realistic plastic human skeleton in its front window, with little red arrows along the spine, all the places where pain might originate.

Hortensia Cervantes jogged across the street and met up with them, saying "Oh, Carraway, I'm so glad to see you!"

She was not breathing hard, for all her exertion. She was wearing an aquamarine sweatshirt and matching pants, with what Nina estimated must be about size four Mizuno athletic shoes. Hortensia managed the local movie theater, which specialized in moody films with subtitles. She liked to talk to her audiences before the trailers began, telling them no outside food was allowed, making it sound like good news.

Hortensia trotted in place on the sidewalk, hurrying without going anywhere while Carraway told her she was looking good.

Hortensia did look good, that much was true. Nina did not feel jealous, exactly, but she was not happy about Hortensia's attention, either. This new, sinewy Carraway looked better than ever, a man with stories to tell.

Terrence had once told Nina that she was intelligent, territorial, and gifted. She had always thought that these were all desirable attributes, but now she wondered— maybe *territorial* simply meant *jealous*. She wished she and her brother could run into someone less flirtatious, one of her personal friends who would not necessarily bat her eyes at Carraway the way Hortensia was doing, bobbing up and down.

But Nina's best friend, Celeste, had moved to Alaska—her father had gotten a job as an environmental engineer, laying ice-melt drainage in the wilderness surrounding Ketchikan. All Nina heard from her friend these days were increasingly short messages. *Nz px* was her response to a series of twilight photographs Nina had emailed her. And a recent e-mail response to Nina's long narrative of a visit to a computer convention in Sunnyvale had read, in total: *?!*

At last Hortensia bounded away up Washington Street, but even then Nina could not be alone with her brother.

A tattered figure on a bicycle hailed Carraway. This was emaciated and ever-cheerful Zebulon, the town derelict. No one knew where exactly Zebulon slept at night, and Nina suspected a refuge in the creek bed or in a hidey-hole in Albany Hill. Zebulon was not a very old man, but he was toothless and haggard, a casualty, Nina believed, of years of hard drugs.

"It's good to see you back, man," said Zebulon.

Carraway asked Zebulon where he was staying these days, and Nina could see why Carraway was good at police work, asking questions, listening carefully to the answers.

"I got a place out by Cerrito Creek that's not too bad," Zebulon replied. "All summer, until it rains."

THE WAITRESS in the Royal Cafe, a woman with a great deal of eye makeup, her red hair gathered into two ponytails, knew Carraway from junior high.

One of the busboys had gone to school with him, too, a stocky guy with a gold tooth, and there was a long moment with people saying how it was good to see him back home. Nina was not surprised how much people liked Carraway.

But she saw that Carraway held back from saying more than he had to, and she wondered if it had been a mistake to come to this well-lit place, a retro diner with people tucking into breakfast burritos.

She wondered, not for the first time, if her father's gourmet shop was a thing of the past. People were weary of balsamic vinegar and French truffles, and what they wanted now was food covered with ketchup. They craved the rough certainty of bologna sandwiches with pickle slices, and beef patties fried hard. They did not want delicate imported spices like fenugreek and lavender. They wanted burritos stuffed with scrambled egg.

Nina had waited while Carraway took a long time to get dressed, pawing through his closet amazed at all the clothes that were his but that he had forgotten. He had, in the end, put on a pair of J. Crew chinos and a leather jacket that looked way too big on him. He wore a pair of Allen Edmonds high-top boots, and only the shoes seemed to belong to him—everything else looked borrowed.

Carraway said he wanted a calm place in the corner of the café, and Nina was not surprised that he wanted his chair edged in as far as it could go into the angle of the walls. He could see everything from there, like a gangster wary of hit men. He ordered the tofu scramble and she ordered a plain omelet.

He didn't talk at all for a long while, and let the food arrive before he even looked like he would ever make a sound. He watched the room before him with a steady caution. He bit the corner off a piece of dry wheat toast.

"So, tell me," she prompted.

"The 649th Military Police Company," Carraway said at last, "provided order and support for a well-organized refugee camp near Basra called Camp Safwan."

She waited encouragingly.

"Most of what we did," he continued, "was arrest people for stealing water pumps and electrical transformers. There wasn't a practical system of jails, and not so much as a kangaroo court, so when we shook down these kids—fourteen-year-old guys, mostly—we let them go. I hated doing that, letting thieves go free. But there was no choice."

"You've always," suggested Nina, "thought bad guys should go to jail."

"Very much so," he agreed with a nod. "Jerry and I often worked as a two-man team, just like civilian cops do. Sometimes, it wasn't what you'd call normal police work. We might be sent out to provide cover, if orders were for an infantry platoon to search a neighborhood for an arms cache.

"There were weapon hoards all over the place. Out in the desert, under people's bedrooms. We carried shotguns, Mossbergs, because with all those civilians around, you didn't want to loose off machine-gun rounds and hurt a bunch of people. I liked the work. But then we went out one evening, when Jerry and I were already tired from a long day, and everything changed."

He looked out at the window across the room, traffic and pedestrians passing by silently.

"We were ordered," he said, "to provide cover for an M1 Abrams tank that had thrown a track—lost one of those tread-belts that make a tank go forward."

She said dryly, "I understand the concept."

He shrugged good-naturedly.

"We went out with several other guys from the same unit," he continued. "We were driving an up-armored Humvee with metal plates all over it, and I was sitting next to the driver. We could see the smoke and headed toward it, a great plume of black pouring up into the sky. Everything in Iraq burns with more smoke than any other place in the world, maybe in history. We could drive off the road, or on the road, it didn't make any difference. The desert there is like a parking lot without any painted stripes, hard surface in all directions."

He looked down at his food.

"By the time our vehicle got out there the tank had taken two rockets," he said, "with bits of tank and projectile fragments all over the pavement."

Maybe, Nina thought, she had been cruel to make him talk about this.

He looked up at her and gave her a reassuring smile.

I'm all right.

But he didn't speak for a long moment.

"I used to be fascinated by tanks," he said, "but when a tank is malfunctioning it's just a helpless container of people. The best way to deploy a tank, in my opinion, is to dig a hole, and bury it up to the turret. But this one was all naked and stuck in a ditch and shot up. In a tank you have a gunner, a driver, a tank commander, and a loader, and in this case the personnel were stricken with BAE—behind armor effects, which is to say they were all dead."

He shook his head as though amazed at his former stupidity, or maybe his foolhardiness.

He looked to one side, as though seeing it all again.

Nina did not want him to see these painful images in his mind, but she kept quiet.

She wanted to know.

13

I volunteered to go down into the tank," Carraway continued, "to verify the status, and I had the idea I could figure out the weapon instructions and get the tank to fire a round or two of artillery, just to help establish the perimeter and buy us some time.

"But the instructions next to the gun breech were stuff like 'normal mode/ammunition select' and my favorite, 'sabot hep,' whatever that means. I was lost in there with four dead guys and then a mortar round came down that blew off the turret hatch. I took a piece of shrapnel down through my stomach and into my guts, and that was my war."

Her omelet was getting cold. She wasn't hungry now anyway. Her eyes were burning, and she was a little surprised that there were tears in them.

THEY DIDN'T TALK for a while, and waited until the waitress took the plates away. Carraway had eaten all of his scrambled tofu, and said it was the best food he had ever tasted.

"Are you going back to Iraq?" she asked.

She was hoping he would say that there was no way.

"If I put in for a disability discharge," he said, "I have to wait months for a decision—there's a massive backup, thousands of cases. If I'm more than thirty percent disabled, I'll get monthly checks for life. But if I'm ten percent disabled they'll give me a severance check and kiss me goodbye."

"You nearly died!"

"The doctors expect a full recovery, and even though right now my stamina is not high, and I still feel like someone who was cut in two and superglued, I think they're right."

"So you're going back," she said, feeling crestfallen.

"Two guys I know personally have shot themselves," said Carraway. "Both of them experienced military men, facing yet another tour of duty. They got back home to Walnut Creek or Turlock, settled in with their families and friends, and looked at the calendar and realized they couldn't return, no matter what."

"That's terrible," said Nina, thinking that *terrible* did not begin to summarize what she was hearing. "But when you think about suicide—isn't it an overreaction?"

"Sure," he said. "It is, no question, an overreaction. But you get used to thinking like that: if you feel anger or you feel guilt, you take the shortest route to solve the problem.

And there's a lot of guilt, when you get back home to Wal-Mart and Burger King. You see things over there, and do things, and when you get back to civilian life you can't live with the memory."

She felt a rush of concern for her brother. "But you wouldn't, Carraway. You would think of—"

Before she could finish her question, he gave her hand a reassuring pat. "No, I wouldn't, Nina. Don't worry. I have other plans."

"Like what?"

"A buddy of mine has a dad who specializes in children's dentistry—a recession-proof income. His dad paid a San Jose attorney named Lowell to cut through the red tape, get him a discharge, and now my friend is coaching Little League."

"Get in touch with Mr. Lowell."

"It won't be easy. The lawyer's so busy he charges a big retainer," said Carraway, "just to talk to one of his associates. I can't afford one hour with him."

"Do you think Leblanc can help?"

"I'll do anything," said Carraway, "to keep from going back to Iraq."

THEY WERE OUTSIDE and walking along San Pablo Avenue before either of them spoke again.

Carraway asked, "Have you seen my black crocodile sneakers?"

"Those Prada shoes someone gave you and they never fit?"

"They fit," he said. "I loved them—you were just envious."

Maybe she had been, a little. "They never really went along with your tough-guy style."

"Have you heard from Jocelyn lately?" he asked.

Jocelyn Hurlow was Carraway's foremost girlfriend, going back a few years. She was a buyer for Bed Bath & Beyond, and always smelled of Vanilla Boogie or Lavender Bingo, whatever body cream was on sale. Jocelyn lived up the street from the Atwoods, and in recent weeks a steady stream of delivery vans had pulled up before the Hurlow two-story. Either Jocelyn was having simultaneous affairs with a parade of electricians, carpet layers, and painters, or she was remodeling her house.

"I see her at Safeway," Nina said, "buying hummus."

Jocelyn was currently dating the assistant manager of the delicatessen department, a muscular man with a trace of an Australian accent. Nina decided this information would hurt Carraway's feelings, so she didn't mention it.

Carraway made a phone call, and to Nina's relief, he did not call Jocelyn. He spoke to someone in Leblanc's office.

He flipped the phone shut and said, "Mr. Leblanc is taking possession of a house on Gateview Street—we'll meet him there in an hour."

Nina had met Leblanc a few times, in the vitamin aisle

of Solano Drugs and in line at the Cerrito Theater, and the fact that he was a likable whirlwind of a man made her feel, ironically enough, uncomfortable. He was likable the way a raccoon might be likable—you enjoyed the guy, but kept an eye on him.

"I wish it rained here in the summer," Carraway was saying as they wandered up the street. "I miss rainy days."

"Me, too."

Nina hated rain, but she felt a longing to agree with her brother on everything.

She realized how important this walk was to him when he spent so long outside the florist, and alongside the vegetarian Chinese restaurant. He enjoyed looking at things, feeling that he was really home, lingering and reaching out to touch his own reflection in the glass.

Brother and sister had turned back, heading toward home, when someone rushed past them from the East Bay Bank, a tall, athletic figure, someone in such a hurry that he nearly stumbled as he rounded the corner.

The muscular figure was masked, and he carried a black garbage bag.

14

For a fraction of a second Milton did not recognize the figure in the rearview mirror when he saw the shape running to get away from the bank.

It was a masked individual, not running but coming on fast, a biped creature that was too fluid, and moving too urgently, to be strictly human. His motion was a rapid stride, like a cartoon of someone hurrying across ice to keep from falling.

Bruce had never moved like this before. Perhaps Bruce was clowning, adopting this mime-show of hurry so that Milton might laugh with relief. He would laugh about this, and very soon. Of course this creature was his brother, and naturally his brother had not robbed the bank after all.

Bruce must have changed his mind. The garbage bag was dangling but looked heavy enough to contain at least some money.

What happened?

The words came out soundless, his voice not able to

actually produce a syllable. The passenger door flung open and Bruce heaved the surprisingly heavy bag into the backseat.

Bruce kept the mask on, his eyes glittering, his entire appearance sinister, a man Milton would have been afraid of if he had not known that this panting stranger, too out of breath to talk, was his own brother.

Bruce slammed the door.

He was saying something, a word of explanation, perhaps. Milton could not understand him.

"Drive!" repeated Bruce through the black knit fabric of the watch cap. The raggedly cut eyehole was tugged too far to one side, and only one eye was able to see.

The engine died.

Milton had put his foot down too hard, and the machinery went dead. Except, at the last instant, as the motor guttered and nearly stopped, he lifted his foot from the gas pedal and the thin, dying source of power returned to full life.

THEY DROVE THREE BLOCKS, and then the money blew up.

The noise was loud, accompanied by a flash that forced Milton to crouch over the steering wheel. Green smoke filled the car's interior, and he found the window crank and worked it, getting a little air into the vehicle as he sped up, trying to get as far away as he could from the smoke that flowed out of the car, along with scraps of paper.

They weren't bits of trash, he realized. They were pieces

of money, currency turned charteuse by the exploding dye pack that had somehow found its way into the swag. The air tasted poisonous, and his eyes stung.

Milton put his head out the side window and took a left turn without even slowing for the stop sign, DayGlo green smoke streaming from the car. Bruce was hanging on to the dash with both hands, and that detail, his brother's skin now lurid green like a bronze figure stained with corrosion, made Milton hopeful that the worst of the explosion was clearing.

But there was a residue on the inside of the windshield. It was with effort that Milton turned back north along the streets that he ordinarily knew well but that now were unknown territory. The Ford streamed smoke like a car on fire.

MILTON PULLED OVER to the curb and told Bruce to get out.

He was beyond being afraid, in an enhanced mental state that was like being an instant mastermind. He wasn't even terribly dismayed at what had to be considered a complete failure. This bank robbery business was hard to learn. Milton was learning. This was just the first try at what he knew was going to be a richly successful criminal career.

His voice was still soundless, and only then did he recognize that the explosion had blunted his hearing.

Bruce was pawing through the lime-colored scraps of paper all over the floor, trying to gather up money that looked remotely negotiable. He gave no sign of being able to hear what Milton was saying.

Milton half-fell out of the car, and hurried over to the passenger side. He opened the door and seized his brother, dragging him from the fuming interior. His brother looked like a soldier camouflaged down to the skin, but his makeup did not hide him—it made him all the more visible. Bruce tugged off the mask and his face was pale and anguished.

"I didn't know," Bruce was saying. Or he was probably saying—it was hard for Milton to tell, his ears ringing and Bruce's voice too hoarse.

"It's OK," said Milton, and he was not simply uttering rote reassurance.

He meant it. They were going to figure this enterprise out and next time was going to be brilliant. The next strategy was going to be much more well-considered, and his new insight into robbery made him feel instantly superior to his former, fully ignorant self.

Milton took his brother by the arm and pulled him along, across a tidy green lawn, and over a white picket fence, Bruce still clinging to the black plastic sack. This much of the day's calamity fell into Milton's escape plan, and Milton took this as a good sign.

The two of them stumbled down a rocky embankment into a creek bed.

The next time, Milton swore to himself, they would go up to one of those armored cars and take the money right out of the thing, before the bank could even get its hands on the stuff.

Naturally, such a crime would take real weapons and maybe another person. At least one more person. But Milton respected his own brainpower. They didn't guard such a heavily armored vehicle for nothing. If a financial institution had money in plenty, imagine what quantities of wealth the trucks that brought the stuff must carry.

A slim trickle of water glittered down through a mess of debris and concrete chunks, and disappeared under the street that crossed overhead some thirty yards away.

What sounded like a siren was wending back and forth through the neighborhoods, and with his hearing returning, Milton could make out the clatter of a helicopter, searching from the sky.

For me and Bruce, Milton knew. It was searching for them.

Milton kept hold of his brother's hand, his gloved grasp gritty and sticky with dye, and the two of them slipped down under the avenue, into the dark.

15

Carraway moved swiftly for a guy who'd been nearly killed three months before, and Nina stayed right with him.

They angled behind a red BMW and watched as the running figure tucked his body into a waiting car. The car took off after a lurching, hesitant start.

Carraway asked, "Do you know what just happened?"

She could guess.

He pulled a cell phone out of his pocket and called 911, sounding like a law enforcement professional, giving the license plate and description of the getaway vehicle. Nina walked up the street and observed the armored car, uninvolved in the robbery, apparently, but sullen and unmoving, like a large, horn-plated creature overcome by caution.

She felt a thrill at seeing a bank robbery take place. A siren was approaching, and was joined by another. No one emerged from the armored car, the wheeled, gray fortress staying right where it was, angled across empty spaces in the bank parking lot.

When the police arrived, Carraway liked talking to them—she could tell by the way he gestured, pointing up Washington Avenue, putting his hands on his hips, the cops fascinated with references to Iraq.

Nina was interviewed by her own cop, a broad-built, well-mannered officer with the name DEAN pinned to his shirt. He was a youthful-looking man, but when she got close to him she could see seriousness in his eyes.

She described what she had seen, a masked sprinter with a black plastic garbage bag.

The bag had not looked all that full. She wondered how much cash the robbers got away with, but she couldn't think of a way to ask without sounding like an aspiring robber.

No one got out of the armored car, but Nina could see the driver on the radio, probably talking to the cops and his dispatcher. The vehicle slowly crossed the parking lot and headed up the street, as if deciding to do business at the bank some other day. Officer Dean followed her gaze and gave a quiet laugh.

"The bank is closed for business," Officer Dean said, "until we finish with the crime scene."

"I guess I won't be able to cash a check."

"The Loomis guys will be back tomorrow, for sure," Officer Dean said, a handsome man when he smiled. "A bank usually loses an entire day when there's a robbery."

The cop closed his notebook, but he didn't turn away, a man too easygoing, Nina thought, to be a tough-guy cop.

He wore a wedding ring, and she felt a pang of concern—there was so much that could go wrong in a policeman's life.

She asked, "How much money do you think one of those armored cars might hold?"

"A lot," he said.

She had to come out and ask. "How much?"

"If the robbers had hit the armored car," said Officer Dean, "they would have gotten away with millions."

"Loomis must have a lot of trouble with robbery."

"There has been a rash of attempts lately," said Officer Dean with an expression of distaste, like a restaurant patron admitting he doesn't like liver. "The armored car company has put out a reward, fifty thousand dollars, for information leading to the arrest of anyone who robs one of their vehicles. And the bank has a seventy-five-thousand-dollar reward for the capture of robbers. We need the public's help these days."

Carraway had overhead the last of Nina's conversation with Officer Dean as he joined them.

Officer Dean shook Carraway's hand. "We prayed for you," he said, and Carraway thanked him.

While Carraway showed no overt interest in religion, Nina knew he kept a notebook of religious quotations in his nightstand. The passages were written out in Carraway's own, draftsman-neat handwriting. *Nor height, nor depth, nor any other creature, shall be able to separate us from the love of God.*

"Do you think you'll catch these robbers?" Nina asked.

A helicopter puttered across the sky, one of the Oakland police choppers the East Bay authorities used when there was trouble.

"Well," said Officer Dean, "these characters don't rob banks because they're clever. No matter how you figure, it's a dumb thing to do."

But he wasn't really paying that much attention to what he was saying, and Nina was partially deaf to his remarks, too, caught by the sight of the circling helicopter.

16

Milton and Bruce splashed along, following the creek bed.

The water was slack, the specter of a stream, diminished by the usual summer drought. The dim current smelled of automobile lubricant, lawn runoff, and dog waste. At times the water flowed along a concrete shelf, when the stream tunneled forward under a street. At other times the water-course was open to the sky, prettily shaded by bay trees, shaggy horsetail reeds along the banks.

They tore off their plastic gloves and discarded them, and before long they had green hands. The green dye smeared all over, and Bruce's face had become as green as the rest of him. The black plastic bag was ruptured and blistered in places, but still largely intact.

Backyard dogs caught their sound as they made their way along the modest flow of water, and most of the dogs barked with great interest, raising an alarm. The helicopter was far behind them, circling in uncertain passes over the strip malls of El Cerrito and the college-town neighborhoods of north Berkeley.

The round opening of another tunnel opened before them, and Milton leaned against the concrete surrounding the gap. This passageway was small, slimed with moss, and dark. Milton could squeeze into it, and make progress, but he was not certain that his larger brother would be able to do the same.

He looked back to see the stained, weary figure of Bruce silently begging for him to stop.

"We're almost home," said Milton.

He was thirsty and needed to stand under a hot shower. A jar of homemade cleaner, their dad's own concoction, waited in the basement—a mixture of detergent, borax, paint thinner, and other chemicals that could clean anything off anything. He wasn't worried about having green skin for the rest of his life.

But he was grateful for a pause, catching his breath and reckoning Bruce's size against the diameter of the corrugated metal passageway.

"I won't fit into that hole," protested Bruce. He was still carrying the black plastic garbage bag, and inside the sack was a large wad of discolored money.

Milton considered this assertion. He was fairly certain that Bruce would fit, but only with determined effort. "You aren't hurt, are you?"

Bruce shook his head and leaned back against a graffiti-decorated embankment, concrete festooned with strands of ivy. Street gangs had left their tags with spray cans, and artists undertook signature designs, mocking faces, starburst scribbles.

"I guess she slipped the thing in at the very end," said Bruce.

Milton told him not to worry about it.

"That brunette with the face like a cat," Bruce persisted. "She put the squib in the bag."

Milton realized that a calm debriefing of the day's misfortune, and a serious discussion of a new plan, was very much a good idea. This was not, however, the best time and place for such a conference.

He said, "Never mind."

" 'Never mind,' " mocked his brother in quiet exasperation. Bruce shook his head, and looked around at the overhanging trees and backyard fences, wood planks painted decades ago and now weathered gray.

Bruce looked back at Milton and his teeth were gleaming within his green mask of a countenance. He was smiling.

"You look funny," said Bruce.

"You look bad, too," said Milton.

The two of them laughed, but quietly.

"I don't want you forgiving me," said Bruce when he could speak again.

Milton felt deep affection for his brother, but every now and then his brother's character was hard to fathom.

"OK," he said tentatively. "No forgiving." He knew his brother needed special handling, and special timing, too, so he waited before he asked, "Why not?"

"Because it's just a way of you acting superior."

"You mean you think I'm being patronizing," said Milton.

"That's what I think."

A siren stitched the murmuring townscape all around them, so distant that the sound was reassuring. The cops had no idea where they were.

"I got over this as soon as it happened," said Milton.

Bruce looked at his brother, not breathing so hard now, calm but weird, with all that dye and mud decorating his anguished form. His hair was a crown of bronze spikes. "How, Milton?" he asked in a tone of hopeful incredulity. "How did you get over this?"

"I instantaneously put the disappointment behind me," said Milton, his mood enlightened by a wise, almost saintly benevolence. "I'm glad you're not hurt."

Bruce sighed, wordlessly acknowledging his brother's concern.

"Besides," said Milton, "I have a better idea."

Maybe Bruce did not take in the words at once. It took him a long moment to ask, "For what?"

Milton had been a little hesitant to broach this fresh

design right then. But he felt the tug of ambition and so he said, just to see how Bruce would react, "How to do it right next time."

"Shut up for a while," said Bruce with a weary laugh.

Milton crawled into the tunnel in advance of his brother, a small, round mouth of daylight far ahead.

17

Milton's fingers slipped off the slick interior, and his dye-grimed Nikes could not find traction.

The darkness had an unclean odor. The struggle through the passageway made a metallic echo, and the ridges of the tunnel were painful under Milton's knees. The wet soaked into his chemical-scented clothing, and he suppressed a shudder brought on by a horror of this place, a sensation of suffocating claustrophobia and rats.

He could smell the rodents. He disliked this tunnel far more than he had anticipated. And as his brother grunted and squeezed through the passage behind him, the round O of daylight far ahead seemed to be growing more distant.

"When we get home," Milton said, his strained voice echoing in the metallic interior, "we bury our clothes and the money." Sometimes, he reasoned, a crisis was diminished by spoken communication.

Time went by with no response, however, so he asked if Bruce understood.

His brother spoke with effort, squeezing his shoulders through the dark tube. "We can wash the money."

Milton wondered if Bruce had heard of money laundering and not grasped the concept. Washing the cash was not a reasonable plan, anyway, because the dye was no doubt permanent, but Milton wanted to be encouraging at this point.

"Sure," he said, reaching and seizing a ridge in the cold aluminum and pulling his body forward. "We can wash the money, if we decide to, but for now the stuff is evidence."

His brother's head bumped the soles of Milton's shoes, the big guy making good progress. The circle of daylight was getting closer just as the constriction of the tube grew worse, months of litter and tree branches choking the passage.

"Next time," said Bruce, "I'm using a real gun."

THE TWO OF THEM crawled out of the tunnel and took deep, relieved gulps of fresh air.

Milton would have felt the beginnings of exaltation, with Albany Hill and home looming nearby, if Bruce had not made a discovery that caused him to become angry.

A makeshift shelter had been set up high along the stream bank, a lean-to of plywood and cardboard, the gaps in the improvised walls closed by wads of trash and rags.

Bruce climbed up the concrete embankment and dropped the sack of money. Then he seized a sheet of plywood and threw it down into the slowly flowing stream.

He dismantled the entire crude homestead, ignoring Milton's protests.

"You can't do that," Milton objected. "That's where Zebulon keeps his belongings." *Belongings* was scarcely the word for such a ragtag assortment, but Milton had a certain regard for the town's foremost oddball.

"He has no right," said Bruce, tossing a sleeping bag down into the creek.

Milton tried to muster a line of argument that would dissuade his brother, but by the time he was ready to contend "Do unto others" it was too late. The makeshift shelter was nearly gone, its remains all over the place.

A cracked voice called out. "Keep your hands off my stuff!"

Zebulon was just arriving. He dragged his bicycle, a rusting ten-speed with worn tires, and then dropped it in his torment, hurrying forward to stand unsteadily between Bruce and what was left of his camping site.

Bruce towered over the emaciated individual, and Milton dreaded a repeat of the crosswalk incident. Earnest action on his part was all that might keep Bruce from seriously injuring someone.

"You have no right, man," continued Zebulon, falling defensively to one knee. Any hint of confidence had vanished from his voice. Bruce bunched his fists and Zebulon moved to protect his body from what was sure to be a blow or a kick.

Milton took Bruce by a discolored sleeve. He pulled his

brother hard, so hard that the two of them would have fallen if they had not found their footing, staggering back down the slope into the streambed.

"No right," called Zebulon as the two brothers left him.

"He was trespassing," Bruce explained to his brother, the brief sentence all he would, for the moment, offer as explanation. He retrieved the bag of money from the side of the creek.

Milton mouthed the word in silent dismay, talking to himself. *Trespassing*. He felt like appealing to an invisible audience regarding his brother. *Can you believe this guy?*

They splashed down the creek for a few moments, and Milton found the deer trail that wended up through the drought-stiffened cattails, the exit out of this watercourse and toward home.

"Calm down," Bruce said, gradually aware that his violence against Zebulon had offended his older brother.

Milton would have liked to have a discussion of his brother's sense of right and wrong, because he did feel that there was a consistency to his brother's view of the world. An exchange of philosophical views would be welcome, on another day.

"All right, I'm calm," Milton snapped.

"Zebulon was trespassing on public property," said Bruce, with the equanimity of a superior court judge.

"We have to climb up this slope to our backyard," Milton replied, not wanting to get into a discussion. "And then what?"

Bruce put a reassuring, grimy hand on his brother's shoulder. "We bury the money. If you still want to do that."

Can you believe this guy?

Maybe, thought Milton, his own half-conceived impulse to destroy Bruce was mirrored by his brother. Perhaps Bruce harbored a half-conscious desire to wreck his brother's hopes. Milton briefly conceived a plan to call Officer Dean anonymously and turn his brother in.

"What are you going to say," prompted Milton, "if we see anyone?"

"I'll act normal."

"You can't act normal, you're covered with green." Milton offered a ragged, exasperated laugh as he spoke, but he could see clearly what was wrong with his life. If he could have Bruce arrested and remain free himself, that's what he would do.

"Tell me," Bruce was saying, patient and compliant. He sounded subtly challenging. "Tell me how to act, Milton."

"Just don't talk," said Milton.

He spaced the words out for emphasis, aware of the distant helicopters that persisted, working their way closer.

Bruce admired his brother, although he was amazed at Milton's indifference to the slights and outrages of life. Bruce did not like to put his impulses into words, but if he had pulled together an explanation for his feelings regarding Zebulon's dwelling place, he would have said that Milton and Bruce did not live like that, squatting on public land, so why should that leathery drug addict get away with such behavior?

Why should sports car drivers think they could lazily breeze through crosswalks, and what made banks think they could sit hunkered down on huge amounts of money with decent people like Bruce's mom barely able to afford cigarettes?

Just don't talk.

As though Bruce was a gofer, a lackey and nothing more. Well, Bruce had a higher sense of proper behavior than most people. He hated public begging, and he recycled cans and bottles he found, like the ones he was picking up now, two Budweiser cans lying there in the reeds.

"We don't have time for that," Milton was saying, looking like a green devil with all that dye.

Someday, Bruce swore to himself, he was going to show Milton what he could do. On that day there would be a serious body count—blood everywhere.

18

Terrence Quinion put on the earphones again.

He could sit in the dry brush like this for hours. There was plenty to listen to, and a recording session in nature was easily as interesting as listening to baseball or football on TV. Also, what he heard was real life. Real hunger, real death.

A wasp sang through the air, a sound like a cello string stroked by a bow, and a hummingbird whipped across his hearing, a current of pure voltage. For a long while there had been helicopters, circling and clattering to the east, but the distracting aircraft were silent now.

He was intending to record the family of red-tailed hawks that lived on the hill, just as he had explained to Dr. Saltz earlier that day. The birds had been hunting all week, joyfully and stridently. The hawk was a triumphant predator with a way of calling out with a half-musical, two-note *skree*, as though simply being an efficient killer was not enough—you had to issue proclamations about what you were doing.

He had given the animals code names. The male was President, because he liked to speak and be heard. The female he had named Donna, because she was like an opera prima donna with her two-note solos. The two juveniles he had dubbed Rookie One and Rookie Two—he could not yet guess their respective sexes.

He was not having any luck recording the sound of the hawks, however—not today. The hawks had a way of confounding whatever Terrence was after. Sometimes the creatures liked to show off, but other times they shut up. President was particularly knowing, and liked to position his gliding flight paths at the very edge of audibility, teasingly, making Terrence work to catch the rumor of a kill.

Terrence was sitting under a tall eucalyptus on Albany Hill, the splashes of early afternoon sun falling across the lenses of his glasses. He had to close his eyes against the glare.

The juncos—small, fast-moving birds—made high-pitched querying sounds. To a human being the darting signal from bush to bush sounded playful, but Terrence believed that with their smaller, hollow bones and relatively tiny ears, the birds heard sounds at a lower, richer level.

In their wild sensitivity, the black-and-white juncos were uttering baritone watchwords, keeping in touch—about Terrence, where he was sitting and what he was doing, and about the hawks. Terrence turned up the volume on the Sony recorder as the quick, unseen creatures gossiped apprehensively and knowingly about their world.

A scrub jay snagged a branch overhead and squalled to the other jays in the vicinity that the human being with the things on his ears was still sitting here. The bird's communication was not particularly fearful. A jay was not afraid of very much, although the approach of a hawk gave them a good deal of good-natured alarm to spread. If an owl chanced to be in the sky when a jay was around, however, the sentinel jay would call out a particularly shrill warning, for every bird of every species to hear. Every creature on the hill was afraid of owls. Even a human could come to understand such a communication—*Death is on the wing.*

Terrence did not believe that humans were incalculably more intelligent than animals. People were adept at maintaining their own organized ways of life, but when you confronted the bright alertness of a jay or a raven you learned a kind of humility. People were smart, but birds were smart, too.

The hawks kept their continuing silence now. The jays hurried off. Terrence waited as before, but he was beginning to believe that something was amiss.

Terrence had what most people considered large amounts of patience, but what seemed like fortitude was the result of his training as someone who could not see well. To get around town, he counted the steps from the sandwich shop to the liquor store, and from San Pablo Avenue to his home.

But something was troubling the bird community of the entire eastern slope of the hill, and even after a long hour of vigil, Terrence got nothing, only ambient noise. He became increasingly curious.

A clank and chime reached him through his earphones, steel against rock, and he made out the sound of two male voices. He could not discern exactly what they were saying, but they were furtive, unhappy, and digging what sounded like a grave in the stony earth of the hillside.

Terrence's mood shifted from curiosity to suspicion.

He knew these voices.

They belonged to two people Terrence always tried to avoid.

19

Terrence put the recorder and the earphones into his backpack and followed the trail downslope with care.

The sounds from the neighborhood were loud once you left the cover of the trees, a car wash and the breathy burr of a street cleaner the loudest noises. And then the sigh of a bus, with its pneumatic brakes, and the ongoing racket of what sounded like a pair of shovels.

Sometimes archaeologists searched the hillside for artifacts of the Native American tribe that had once lived there, along the shores of Cerrito Creek, and ancient graves had been uncovered. But these two were not scientists, Terrence knew, and he made his way cautiously between the scarlet-leaved poison oak and the sprawling native oaks along the trail.

No doubt a wiser or more practical individual would have passed on by, and Terrence considered minding his own business, but something was wrong, and he wanted to find out what it was.

Soon he reached the foot of the hill.

He tried to come up with a good opening line, something disarming. The best he could do was, "Hello there, Milton."

"Oh, Terrence," said Milton, breathing hard. He did not sound pleased.

Sunlight glinted off what must have been a shovel blade. Bruce was a blurred shadow, in Terrence's eyes, barely perceptible and not saying a word.

"Up recording birds and bugs," said Milton, "aren't you?"

Terrence said, "That's right." He made an effort to look at their faces, judging as well as he could where their eyes must be. Dr. Chung, his counselor at the high school, had explained how important eye contact—pretend eye contact in Terrence's case—was in conversation. *Look like you're looking* had been his advice.

Terrence did not like the Borchards. Even their name had a rawboned, harsh quality—*bore-churd*.

The late Mr. Borchard had poisoned dogs, including a beloved rottweiler named Clem that had belonged to the Hathaway family. Bruce was a school dropout, and was rumored to be a construction worker with a firm that buried dead bodies in concrete. Milton had been the sort of student who was always being called out of class to be questioned about shoplifting and vandalism but who never got caught.

"What kind of bird are you recording today?" Milton asked.

"The hawk," replied Terrence, habitual good manners prompting him to add, "Tonight I'll be on the hill recording that great horned owl we've all been hearing."

Terrence was at the back end of the Borchard property, where a rickety fence was slumping under the weight of bindweed and blackberries. He was protected from any possible physical assault by this blur of vegetation.

"I've heard that bird, too," said Bruce, breaking his quiet.

Milton must have given Bruce a silencing glance— Terrence could not observe the moment, but he sensed Bruce's effort to shut up.

"We're digging," said Milton.

"The ground here is all basalt," said Terrence. "Unbreakable rock. Tough going."

"Tell me about it," said Milton in full agreement.

"You haven't murdered anyone, have you?" asked Terrence.

Milton laughed, but Bruce made no additional sound.

"I was joking," said Terrence, because with the Borchards you never knew how they would respond to a remark.

"Just working on a posthole," said Milton. "Maybe about to decide we need a post auger, or some dynamite."

Milton had set the Albany High cafeteria Dumpster on

fire with a string of firecrackers one lunch hour, although of course the school authorities had never been able to pin the crime on him. Terrence was not surprised to hear the Borchards were about to improve their property with explosives.

Milton's color was not right, Terrence felt as he stepped to one side and lifted his hand against the sunlight. Why would Milton be such a bizarre green hue? It was easy for Terrence to doubt visual evidence. But the two brothers gave off a strange odor, too, a sulfuric, chemical smell.

"But just so you know, even if we haven't actually wasted someone, we are practicing," said Milton.

"Practicing?" Terrence asked, not liking the new, unsettled sound in Milton's voice.

"In case we have to do it for real." Milton laughed, like he was telling a funny story.

"So you would know how," said Terrence, playing along with the troubling comedy in Milton's voice.

"That's right," said Milton. "So if someone said they had seen us digging on our property, Bruce could stuff them head down in the dirt."

He offered this as though he was still joking, but Terrence heard the threat.

20

A breath of water from a lawn sprinkler touched Terrence's cheek as he hurried home. Major Wanstead called out a greeting, and Terrence looked in his direction, able to make out a gray-haired haziness in the sunlight.

"How's it going there, Terrence?" came the salutation.

Terrence's difficulties made it just a little hard to know how to respond to simple social remarks. He could not read people's expressions and judge how interested they really might be in the progress of his day.

"It's going all right," said Terrence.

He shifted the backpack with its recording equipment to his other shoulder—he did not want water soaking into the electronics. The sprinkler created a vast plume that caught the sunlight, and the drops made crisp, individual patters on the Bermuda hybrid.

"Another beautiful day," said Major Wanstead, and Terrence felt the need in the man, the yearning for conversation, with nothing but monotonous weather to discuss.

Major Wanstead had been in the Gulf War, and had a military man's way of dealing with matters. He was a man with hunting rifles and a collection of DVDs about warfare, and he spent hours policing his lawn and troweling his bed of nasturtiums. He suffered from a tremor in his hands and chronic weariness, the aftereffects of the war, and was often featured on the Web and in the news, as a local expert on government neglect of veterans.

What I need, thought Terrence, is a man like this retired army officer to tell me how to deal with the Borchards.

As TERRENCE APPROACHED his own home, a woman bustled down the path from the front steps and said, in a tone of heartfelt finality, "Terrence, I've enjoyed knowing you."

Deirdre Howard was all earrings and bracelets. Terrence could make out the rich earth hues of a billowing blouse, and full sleeves, with something bright around her middle, maybe a linked silver belt. She sounded intense and unhappy.

"Have you and Mother had a—" He searched for the right word. "A misunderstanding?"

"A difference of opinion." She gave the words some backspin, meaning that she was deeply offended. Deirdre rummaged in her purse, and Terrence could make out a Kleenex. The woman touched it to her eyes.

"I admire your mother so much," said Deirdre, in a tone that contradicted her statement. And then she was gone, a vague vision, bangles and fabric.

Terrence was glad to be home.

"How was dear Dr. Saltz?" his mother asked.

Annette Quinion asked the same question the same way every six months.

Terrence let the front door shut behind him, and even though it was afternoon and a bright and peaceful day out he worked the dead bolt, locking the entrance. He wanted to feel safe.

The house was filled with a collection of art and artifacts Annette had purchased from clients over the years. The dwelling was small, like most homes in the neighborhood, but the design had been inspired by Anglo-colonial two-stories of another era, and the interior felt more spacious, with its hardwood floors and sweeping banister, than it really was.

His mother was good at what she did. When people died their families were often left with a house full of possessions, some valuable, most not. A liquidation service arranged and advertised open houses, and invited the public for bargain prices on everything from kitchenware to artwork.

Organization was her strength, keeping track of receipts, computer passwords, and who owed her money. Terrence leaned over her papers and files, trying to see what she was organizing today. Her business cards had momentarily scattered all over the shiny dark surface of the table. He knew what they said without actually reading them. *Annette Quinion, estate realization.*

When she was considering the name for her business, Terrence had suggested Squid Liquidators or Grab and Go. But Annette was a woman who did things with a degree of style. Other liquidation services propped tawdry sandwich boards on the corner, and stapled bright flyers on telephone poles. Loot! and Pretty and Cheap, business names without a trace of good taste.

Now she gathered up the stray business cards and slipped a rubber band around them—she hated messy papers. Terrence liked the way the rubber band sounded, a high, ascending scale of notes as she secured the cards. He could not quite see what she was dealing with on her laptop now: a picture of what he took to be a horse's head.

"A family is selling their horse?"

The query was not unreasonable. Golden Gate Fields was a Thoroughbred racetrack at the Albany shoreline, and the town was accustomed to heavy traffic during racing season and wranglers and jockeys queuing at Max's Liquors.

"This is a Tang-dynasty statuette, fifteen hundred years old," she said. "I'm appraising it myself, online. Deirdre ripped me off last month with those cowboy etchings."

"Deirdre says she admires you," said Terrence. He liked to share a compliment, and his mother usually liked hearing them.

But his mother did not reply.

He said, "I actually sort of like Deirdre, in a way."

This drew his mother's curiosity, and her suspicion. "You like her?"

"Sort of."

Deirdre was an art appraiser who claimed a 20 percent cut if an item she had valued sold. The arrangement sounded fair, because Deirdre often provided assistance at no cost.

But last week's prints of bucking broncos and cowboys with their Stetsons flying into the air had been valued by Deirdre at a hundred thousand dollars, and Deirdre had sold them to a friend of a friend before the actual estate sale was scheduled. The art was immediately reported as stolen, and Annette suspected an inflated price and a finder's fee from the buyer, all under the table and in addition to the check she had to write for Deirdre's services.

"Deirdre is a crook, as I have discovered too late," his mother said. "But the insurance company can find that out for themselves."

His mother made a patting gesture on a sofa cushion, and Terrence sat.

She inquired again about Dr. Saltz, and Terrence was aware that he did not want to bring up the subject of eyesight and medical treatment with the tone of acrimony and mistrust lingering in the room.

"Remember," said Terrence, "how Dr. Saltz said that someday we might begin to be able to consider an operation?"

21

"Surgery?" his mother prompted, sounding startled—but instantly hopeful, too.

He nodded.

"Oh!" She could not speak for a moment. "That's good news, Terrence." She reached for his hand, squeezing it too hard. "Isn't it?"

She had a way of overreacting, and he wished now that he had crept up on the subject, maybe talking about how BART had been crowded, how he'd helped a Polish family needing directions to the Oakland Museum.

"Corrective surgery," he said, "to fix my eyes."

"Yes! Well! We always knew the day would come, right?"

"I guess."

Annette and her business suffered through long seasons when not enough people died and the need for liquidation professionals was diminished. Paying a publicist to update her Web site meant that they had to eat Wheaties for supper, and she altered the ever expanding and diminishing waistlines of her clothing with a needle and thread, rarely able to afford a trip to Nordstrom.

"Your father will help pay, don't worry about the money," she was saying, and Terrence said that he had not been worried at all, a perfect falsehood.

If his mother had been a calmer individual, with less on her mind, he would have mentioned the Borchards. But now he felt that he had to protect her from even thinking about Milton and Bruce. Besides, he was not sure what he had witnessed. A call to the police would probably be a waste of everyone's time, and a patrol car parked at the curb would draw the attention of the two brothers.

"Remember," she said, "you wanted me to help you with the owl tonight."

"Who could forget?"

"I'm counting on it," she said.

Annette took a keen interest in Terrence's bird recordings, in part because she had appeared in the Sunday *Chronicle* article about her son's contract with Lucasfilm.

At first Terrence had suspected that she was exaggerating her enthusiasm, as a way of encouraging her son, or perhaps she hoped to get into the newspaper again. But she kept a tally of birds they had recorded, from the hummingbird to the towhee, and she had bought him a new heavy-duty flashlight at Ace Hardware, along with a belt holster to hang it from. He had heard her on the phone, telling a friend that they recorded a late-season crowned sparrow "with the sweetest song I've ever heard."

Terrence appreciated her help at night, when he could easily wander off into the undergrowth. And she was right about the crowned sparrow, an underrated songster if there ever was one.

What Terrence wanted to do someday was create a piece of music that was all birdsong, not just a couple of minutes' worth, but an entire symphony-length work. Another exciting possibility was to make a series of recordings of birds imitating other birds. The scrub jay could do a brilliant knockoff of the red-tailed hawk call, and the starling could sound much like a quail.

Terrence made his way upstairs to his bedroom. The walls were covered with examples of Nina's pictures, and by stepping up close to them Terrence could enjoy the photographs, the Bay Bridge at night, blazing with taillights, and downtown Oakland looking uncharacteristically romantic in the rain.

He used his desktop computer to listen to the recording he had just made on Albany Hill. Once again he heard the clink of shovel against stone, and the drone of the Borchards' voices. Terrence filtered out the susurration of the wind, and he turned down the volume on the twittering juncos and the querying chickadees, enhancing the sound of the two of them.

He was hoping to catch an incriminating remark, a spy-movie clue, but all he heard was a vague impression of words and heavy breathing, nothing distinct. The obscure sounds of the Borchards came out of the two speakers on his desk, an unpleasant presence in the room.

Bruce's voice could be made out saying, "We can put a new roof on the garage," and aside from breathy complaints about the surprising warmth of the afternoon sun and the ineffectiveness of the shovel, that was all Terrence could glean.

He sat on his bed as he checked on text messages on his cell phone.

There was one from Nina, all exclamation points and excitement.

Carraway is back!!!

22

Carraway was starting to get tired, the hitch in his stride becoming more pronounced.

For this reason Nina drove their father's Saab to the meeting with Leblanc, even though the house Leblanc was repossessing was on the west side of Albany Hill, less than a mile away.

The dwelling on Gateview Street was all glass, with a few metal supports for the roof, and had a view of the racetrack and San Francisco Bay, with the Golden Gate Bridge to the west. The bridge was framed by the marine layer of clouds that seethed offshore. On the bay a container ship hulked south, past the docks of San Francisco.

A man in a dark suit and sunglasses stood in the driveway, and he stepped over to intercept Nina and her brother as they approached the house.

"Mr. Leblanc expects us," said Carraway.

The security man's sunglasses were the reflecting type, two convex mirrors. The reflections showed Nina with her short hair and Ray-Bans and Carraway squinting like he wished he had brought a pair of sunglasses himself, both of them distorted caricatures in the guard's lenses.

The guard had lines on his cheeks, the seasoned look, Nina thought, of years of stakeouts and target practice. She tried to picture the guard laughing at a joke, or maybe naked in his shower. She couldn't.

"CARRAWAY, you look fantastic!" said Leblanc.

Carraway said, "I'm not doing too bad."

The house Leblanc had repossessed was roomy, with the smell of fresh paint. There was no furniture, and protective plastic lanes had been taped across the new carpeting. Their feet made distracting rustling noises on the translucent surface.

"You lost some weight," said Mr. Leblanc. "Got a little rest in the hospital, I bet, getting ready to go back and kick some terrorist butt."

Philip Leblanc was a short, square man, with a quick smile and warm handshake. He was dressed in an open-collar white shirt and a sports jacket, light tan pants, and a pair of highly polished black loafers.

She felt his eyes give her a quick up-and-down, appraising. He winked at her.

Nina didn't exactly appreciate this, but she felt strangely unoffended, the man's ebullience hard to disregard. She was glad that she was wearing a forest-green silk blouse, bought when she could afford such things, and a pair of silk denims that just by accident fit her like tailor-mades. And maybe her death-row haircut wasn't as bad as she feared.

But still—a wink. Leblanc was pushy, cocky. He had what her mother probably would have called a lot of nerve. Nina did not exactly smile back.

"Nina's a beauty," said Mr. Leblanc.

"Sure," said Carraway. He said this not as though good looks were a pleasing feature, or a matter of opinion, but as though her attractiveness was characteristic, like being tall or short, no big deal.

"Do you mind if I get to the point?" continued Carraway.

Leblanc gave an openhanded gesture. "Why not?"

"I'm asking you to do one of two things," said Carraway. "Either hire me back, or loan my father some money."

"Ah," said Leblanc.

"I can detail my father's assets," said Carraway. "And I can assure you that we'll pay back the funds."

Leblanc was not smiling now, but looked preoccupied and regretful.

"You wouldn't need to advance us an entire sum all at once," said Carraway.

Leblanc made a short, dry laugh, not an expression of humor or happiness, but a way of punctuating the conversation, switching from cordial to something altogether different.

"Where," he asked, "is your father now?"

"He's in Italy."

"Refinancing that loan he has with the distributors," said Leblanc. "Or trying to."

He probably did not know this for a fact—he was just making a smart and accurate guess.

Carraway gave a nod. "That's right."

"If he defaulted on a loan to me, I'd take over his business," said Leblanc. "Your father's line of work would be a very pleasant sideline. I could import olive oil and Chianti and write off my expenses, lose money on purpose, pay lower taxes."

Carraway spoke evenly, keeping the emotion out of his voice. But Nina could tell that he was not pleased, the words coming out tense. "The business was my father's dream."

Theodore Atwood had wanted to succeed where his own father had failed—doing something glamorous and stylish in the world of cuisine. Nina's grandfather had been fluent in Italian, French, and classical Greek. He had driven a produce truck for Lucky market, unloading crates of cauliflower, hating his job until an aneurysm killed him. His widow had a master's in philosophy. She smoked Kools and drank straight gin, and wrote recipes for women's magazines. *Chicken cacciatore without all the fuss.* She had died when Nina was eight years old. Her father had inherited a bright, tense, energetic constitution, and Nina was afraid he, too, was destined for an early grave.

"This house," Leblanc was saying, gazing around at the broad glass windows and the sweeping views, "was a family's dream, too. I'm just suggesting what could happen."

Carraway folded his arms at this remark, and Nina could see the alteration in Carraway's outlook begin at that moment. Leblanc was already signaling what the answer would be, and Carraway was ready to be disappointed.

But she knew her brother well. She saw by the way he cocked his head and changed the subject. Carraway was already absorbing what was likely to be bad news, and taking his next mental step.

"You changed decorators," said Carraway.

"I had to, really. Dennis Marchmont was in love with the color gray," said Leblanc. "Gray in all its variations. Off-white, charcoal, ash, all those airy versions of overcast skies. I like color. I let him move on to another project."

"You decided," said Carraway, "that maybe pastels were the smart choice."

"This is fawn blue," said Leblanc. "What do you think?"

"High-quality latex," said Carraway.

"Nina," said Leblanc, "what do you think?"

Nina had the impression that only unborn fawns, or dead ones, were likely to be blue. She didn't want to discuss interior decoration. She kept her voice just as steady as Carraway's, maybe even steadier, looking right at Leblanc.

She said, "You aren't going to give my brother back his job, are you?"

23

Leblanc laughed unhappily, and he made a palms-up *You got me* gesture of surrender.

"You figured Carraway was dead, is my guess," she continued. "You assumed you wouldn't have to see him again, and so you hired someone else."

"Nina, you offend me," said Leblanc. He sounded genuinely hurt.

Carraway gave Nina a hard glance, but he didn't tell her to shut up.

"Carraway, I'm glad you're in one piece," added Leblanc. "Honestly, in my heart. You know that. And when you get your health all the way back, a few months, maybe we can have lunch."

Carraway's mouth set in a thin line.

Leblanc told Nina, "I love your brother."

"Love is important," said Carraway. "But I was hoping for something more material. Some paychecks, for example, so I could afford a lawyer and stay out of Iraq."

Leblanc looked almost sad as he put his hands in his pockets and shrugged. "I'm getting married," he said.

"Congratulations," said Carraway, no joy in his voice.

"It's a big deal, getting married," said Leblanc. "You form an accord, two people, with shared assets."

"That's not a very romantic way of looking at it," said Carraway.

"Her name is Maria," said Leblanc, "and she's my entire life now."

"That's wonderful," said Nina, meaning it. She couldn't help herself. The man seemed pleased, and she felt happy for him.

"But it changes things for me," said Leblanc. "I take better care of myself. I have a new set of guardians, Blue Mountain Security. They guarantee against loss and personal bodily harm if I follow their instructions. I don't like them, it's like being protected by the living dead, but my insurance company insists."

"The bodyguard looks very impressive," said Carraway, sounding, Nina thought, unimpressed.

"I drive a new bulletproof Mercedes," continued Leblanc, "because my health coverage and personal property premiums went through the roof without one."

"We saw the vehicle out front," said Carraway. "Nice-looking."

"My problem is, I'm tied up financially, plenty of money but nothing liquid." Leblanc sounded regretful, and suddenly weary. "Not only that, the IRS is squeezing the blood out of my body on a daily basis."

"Make it clear for me, Mr. Leblanc," Carraway persisted. "I just want you to spell it out. Is there no way at all that you can help my family?"

24

The afternoon was cool, the breeze edging in off the bay. Leblanc stood at the front door, a cordial host waving goodbye.

The new, secure, silver Mercedes was parked at the curb.

"What's so high-security about this car?" asked Nina.

"Not much. It's probably got antimine flooring," Carraway said, "And run-flat tires. A couple of juvenile insurgents could blow it to junk."

She had mentioned the car as a risk-free subject. She was trying to sense how he felt, but Carraway's manner hid his emotion.

So now she asked, "Are you disappointed?"

"Yes," he said. "Very. And I'm surprised."

The security guard detached his figure from beside the tall column of a juniper tree and sauntered toward them, trying to get into earshot. Nina was aware that she and her brother looked unhappy, and potentially dangerous.

"And I'm mad," said Carraway.

They got into the Saab and fastened their seat belts.

"Mr. Leblanc likes you," said Nina.

"He likes you, too," said Carraway, rolling down the side window, "but I can't cash you at the bank."

Nina started the car, but let the engine idle.

He put his hand on the dash, and for the first time she could see the depth of his anger, his finger digging hard into the resilient covering.

"What do you know," he asked, "about armored cars?"

"Not a lot," she said. "Why?"

"I'm just wondering."

She laughed. "We're not going to rob an armored car."

"No, not really. But it's a thought. There's a lot of cash money out there, just out of reach."

"Forget that thought." She tried to sound unconcerned, but she wondered. What was her brother really like now? Was he the sort of war veteran you heard about, hard and embiterred, potentially violent?

The dents his fingers had made in the dashboard were slow to vanish.

"I know guys who used to work for Loomis and Brink's," he said, "before they enlisted. An armored car like the one at the bank is a 4700-series International truck with custom armor. You have two people in the front with handguns, and a man inside the vault with a shotgun. They have polycarbonate-layered glass windshields, just like Mr. Leblanc's new Mercedes."

"That's what I mean—it's too difficult. And it's a job for theives, Carraway. We aren't criminals."

"But if you interrupted a robbery that was in progress," he said, "you'd collect a healthy reward."

"How would you manage that?" she asked.

He took his time, thinking.

She drove to the cul-de-sac at the end of the street. Eucalyptus trees towered over the pavement. She backed the car around but did not proceed, letting the smell of the trees drift in from the open window beside her brother.

She stalled the engine, shifting gears too suddenly.

"You would need a team that was expendable," Carraway was saying as she gunned the engine and powered the car around the corner, along the outskirts of Albany Hill.

"Expendable?" she asked, afraid she understood his meaning.

"Guys you wouldn't be that unhappy," said Carraway, "if they were killed."

"There aren't people," she protested, "who are disposable, like paper plates."

The Saab approached an intersection, and she slowed to a stop.

"You have lived your life," said Carraway, "protected like this." He held out his hands cupped to protect something invisible.

"But people aren't trash," she said.

"You're right," said Carraway. "But I counted on Mr. Leblanc and I came away with nothing."

Before Nina could tell him how relieved she was to hear that he was not about to turn to a life of crime, a car pulled up behind them, the driver leaning on his horn.

"Do you want me to go back and teach the driver some good manners?" asked Carraway. "Maybe hurt him a little?"

"What I want," said Nina, "is for you to stop talking like that."

"Do I scare you?" he asked.

"Yes, you do."

"Sometimes," he said, sounding grave, "I scare myself."

25

Terrence sat on Nina's front steps, letting the afternoon sounds wash over him.

Someone had a basketball and was bouncing the thing with a joyful relentlessness, and way up the street a guy with a drum kit was working on his proficiency with the hi-hat, the jazzy syncopation reaching all the way through the murmur of traffic.

Sparrows celebrated the afternoon, squabbling and questioning, and a robin somewhere made that call that reminded Terrence of a weird laugh, unearthly and sure proof that birds have a great deal to say.

Terrence had called Nina and told her he'd meet them here, and she said they were on their way to a meeting with Mr. Leblanc, giving the man's name a certain turn, like he was an illustrious gangster. But her voice had been strained, and when he inquired he had gotten an imprecise story about a bank robbery and a nice cop and an armored car.

Terrence planned to visit the gallery with Nina that afternoon—he had helped her pick out the pictures she was including in her portfolio. He was excited and anxious about her prospects.

Terrence was excited, too, about Carraway's safe return, and he was eager to be with the two of them, but this was not the first time he had been aware of her laconic older brother as something other than a constructive force.

Certainly Carraway had always been pleasant, in a concise, smooth-mannered way, knowledgeable and attentive, and Terrence wanted to hear about the war in Iraq. But he was aware, too, of a circumspection that he felt when he remembered Carraway, a man who had come back on leave from Camp Roberts with his new, short-short haircut and with offhand talk of banana clips and hand grenades.

Maybe he was simply jealous of Carraway, resentful for the reverent tone in Nina's voice when she spoke about getting another terse e-mail from him. Or maybe her voice today had sounded happy but uneasy, the way she had often sounded when she spoke about her brother.

The Saab purred up the driveway, and there Nina was, swimming through the blurred uncertain tapestry of colors and shapes into his circle, his visible world. Terrence put his arms around her, but she was tense and preoccupied, her shoulder blades sharp through her blouse.

He shook Carraway's hand, feeling the absence of something in the man, and the presence of a new roughness, an unusual sound in his voice. Terrence had expected an alteration—the man had been seriously wounded. But he was very nearly a stranger.

"I recorded some birds on my iPhone for you, Terrence," said Carraway, "but they were only carrion crows."

This was, Terrence thought, an odd remark to make, after a year and a half of absence. The meaning was clear, and unpleasant: While Terrence had been recording the songbirds, Carraway had seen death.

26

They sat and talked in the Atwood living room, a domestic space Terrence had always liked, in part because the furniture was always in predictable places. Annette was always bringing home Navajo pots and Morris chairs, objects for Terrence to sidestep, with difficulty.

Terrence sipped a glass of grapefruit juice Nina had brought him from the kitchen, and he heard all about the robbery as she sat beside him on the sofa. The story was told in Nina's distinctive looping narrative manner—out of sequence, starting with Officer Dean and ending after a dramatic near-encounter with a fleeing robber.

Carraway said little, sitting there so still and quiet that, in Terrence's eyes, he became invisible.

Terrence recounted the events of his own afternoon, including the strange manifestation of the two brothers, delving at the foot of Albany Hill like two demons in a medieval print.

He enjoyed telling his story, and he liked the way Carraway and Nina listened, not making tense little noises the way his mother usually did, but soaking in every detail in captivated silence.

"What color are the dye packs," concluded Terrence, looking toward Carraway, "that tellers slip into money?"

"Glowing green, apparently," said Carraway.

"The trouble is," Terrence continued, "legally speaking, I'm not really a very good witness."

"But you have excellent color awareness," said Nina.

He took her hand.

"What I'm wondering," Terrence said, "is if I should call the police?"

"All the Borchards would need," said Carraway, "is an alibi, what they were doing this morning."

"The police could find what they buried," said Nina.

"There's no probable cause," said Carraway, "that would allow a judge to sign a search warrant."

"I don't want the police going to question the Borchards," Terrence said, "unless they take them away in handcuffs."

"Are you afraid of the Borchards?" asked Carraway.

Terrence did not want to acknowledge cowardice.

"I have to protect my mom," he said. And then he admitted, "I'm not happy about bumping into them again if they think I called the cops. Sure, no question—they scare me."

"Didn't Bruce," asked Carraway, "nearly drown someone in the Albany High pool?"

"A couple summers ago—the police called it mutual combat," Terrence recalled. "The guy was horsing around when Bruce was swimming laps. Bruce likes things to be by the book."

"And I heard Louella Borchard broke a guy's jaw in a bar in Port Costa," said Nina. "He flirted with her in a way she didn't like very well."

"How'd she do that?" asked Terrence.

"She hit him with a barstool," Nina said.

"Does she seem that strong?" Terrence was impressed, but slightly incredulous, and even alarmed. Did people really go getting into violent scrapes like that? The Borchards were even worse than he had thought.

"On a good day she looks tough but pretty," said Nina. "One time I slipped and fell in the rain outside the Solano Grill, right when she was passing me on the sidewalk. She leaned over and picked me up with one hand and said, 'Honey, are you hurt?' "

"I thought she had bad lungs," said Terrence.

"Weak lungs," said Nina, "but everything else is in shape."

"But there might be an innocent explanation," said Carraway. "Where was this stuff being buried?"

Terrence described the setting, out where the half-wild vegetation of Albany Hill met the disorder of the Borchard property line.

"I know where that is," said Carraway. "Out by that big blackberry patch."

"That's the place," said Terrence.

"How big is Bruce Borchard?" asked Carraway.

"He's grown up a lot," said Nina, "since you saw him."

"As big as the guy we saw running from the bank?"

"Probably," said Nina.

"How about what's-his-name, Milton?" asked Carraway. "Has he grown up big and strong, too?"

"No," she said. "Milton is smaller, with a face like a ferret. You know—pointy and sly."

"I like ferrets," said Carraway.

"I don't think you'd like Milton," was her response.

Carraway excused himself and left the room.

"How does he seem to you?" asked Nina in a low voice.

"Calm, alert—the standard-issue Carraway," said Terrence.

"He doesn't seem changed?"

"Well, he's a little different, but what do you expect? Did the two of you have—" He didn't want to say *a fight*. "An argument?"

"With Carraway, you can't be sure," said Nina. "He had a disappointment today with his old boss."

"He needs a long rest," Terrence suggested. "Maybe seeing carrion crows—" He paused.

"Eating dead people," said Nina, with a trace of Carraway's flatness.

"Well, that must be upsetting."

Nina said, "I used to know him like my own mind. But now—"

"Now?"

"Now I'm worried about him."

WHEN CARRAWAY was back in the room, Terrence heard the sounds of an automatic being loaded or unloaded, heavy, metallic clicks he recognized from movie sound tracks. The subtle but precise sounds were unsettling, and he felt Nina stiffen.

"You left the safety off, Nina," said Carraway, "and a round chambered. Not exactly a good example of firearm security."

"Where are you going with the gun?" asked Nina. Terrence could hear the strain in her voice.

"I thought I'd go take a look at the neighborhood," said Carraway.

"I don't think you need to take a nine-millimeter," said Nina, in a tone of forced humor, "to drop by Burger Depot."

"I'm going to go see Jocelyn," said Carraway. Terrence could make out the soft, leathery whisper of a holster.

"She has a new boyfriend," said Nina, "from Sydney, with a neck this big around."

"I'll shoot him," said Carraway.

He laughed after he said this, but after a pause that Terrence thought was uncomfortably long.

"She has new carpet, too, I think," she added. "I bet she makes you take your shoes off."

"That shouldn't be a problem," he said. "And later on this evening, I'll go do a little investigating on the Borchards' property."

"I don't think you can trust the Borchards," said Nina.

"To do what?" asked Carraway.

"To cooperate in trying to rob an armored car," said Nina, "so you can arrest them and cash an even bigger reward check. If that's what you're thinking."

Carraway gave a quiet, nearly silent laugh. "Thanks to your friend here," said Carraway, "I have a better plan. How does half of seventy-five thousand dollars sound to you, Terrence?"

NINA HURRIED AFTER HIM and stopped Carraway on the walkway, where the erstwhile gardener had spread pea gravel and put in place pretty concrete stepping-stones. Now dandelions flowered where the surface used to be raked smooth.

Terrence drifted out onto the front porch and waited there, shielding his eyes against the sunlight, trying to make out where they were. He could not hear what they were saying.

The mid-afternoon sun was bright on a FedEx truck cruising up the street.

"Leave them alone, Carraway," she said, shielding her eyes from the sunlight.

"Why, Nina, are you scared of the Borchards, too?" her brother inquired.

I'm afraid of you, she nearly said.

Nina watched him meander up the street, limping slightly. He put his hand to the place just behind his hip, where he carried the Beretta, making sure the weapon was safe and snug.

Terrence joined her on the walkway and asked her what was wrong.

Nina mentally experimented with telling him, but what was there to tell?

Surely Carraway was joking.

And if he wasn't, Nina got a certain reluctant thrill at the thought of Carraway doing harm and getting his hands on some reward money. After all, Carraway had survived a mortar shell.

He was hard to kill.

27

They were nearly late to Nina's appointment.

They took BART to the Rockridge station, and then did the pedestrian hustle down toward Oakland, past shops selling items like leather trousers and antique lap desks. The climate was warmer here. Bare-chested men with tattoos loaded furniture and women in shorts watched their own reflections in shop windows.

Terrence helped Nina by carrying her portfolio, and by making reassuring remarks, how everything was going to be great.

The large, canvas-strapped folder of photos was fuller than she had realized, and the sidewalks more crowded than she had expected, and she knew she had been a fool to get this far, idiotically optimistic and without any chance of being taken seriously.

She had changed clothes before leaving, into what she thought of as her interview outfit, a matching blouse and skirt in slate blue. But the shoes that went best with the outfit could not be walked in farther than down the hall to the ladies' room, and her two pairs of running shoes were lavender and yellow. At last she had unearthed a pair of sensible flats that she had outgrown but that responded to some shoe polish.

And then there had been a long bout in the mirror, in growing awareness that her burn-victim hairstyle was really not fit to be seen. It was too late for her to drop by Prince Hairy—the cut-rate salon on Shattuck Avenue—and get her hair buzz-cut. Why not? She couldn't look any worse.

"You look fantastic," Terrence said as they bustled down the street.

Nina said, "Well, at least my myopic boyfriend thinks I'm all right."

They had to be buzzed into the Gilliam Gallery—the place had two steel-mesh-and-glass doors and a security camera. The buzz mechanism that released the latch was loud, and didn't work at first. She took the portfolio off Terrence's shoulder, so she could be seen arriving with her own work in hand, and the contents of the folder had shifted, the portfolio hanging awkwardly off her arm.

Her first impression was: quiet.

Very quiet. They entered a room that was mostly silent, empty space, with prints on the wall that looked, to Nina, like checkered tablecloths rendered in varying colors, chartreuse and pink, black and pink, with baby-doll pink showing up in most of the prints.

Pink was not one of Nina's favorite colors. The shade reminded her of human insides, and scar tissue.

Terrence stepped close to several of the artworks in turn, studying them.

The receptionist, who could not have been much older than Nina, was asking her if they needed help.

Nina identified herself, saying that she had a three-thirty appointment, but the artwork she saw around her, and the peculiar absence of sound from the outdoors, made Nina feel as though no sound was coming out of her mouth.

The receptionist smiled. She had small teeth and large gums, and her artificially colored red hair was cut straight across, a comic-book hairstyle Nina admired without really wanting to look exactly like that herself. The receptionist wore skull earrings—little human heads the size of walnuts.

"Please don't stand so close to the art," the receptionist told Terrence.

She smiled again, and Nina thought that sitting in this gallery might be a lonely experience, especially wearing an expensive, big-sleeved blouse, some sort of dark, witchy crepe, that showed the comic-book girl's figure. Nina wondered if Terrence could see well enough to realize that the receptionist was attracted to him, giving him an eye-batting stare.

"I'm practically legally blind," said Terrence, stepping away from the art as directed.

This was not the first time that Nina had heard Terrence refer to his less than adequate vision as though he could turn it to his advantage, maybe even the beginning of a flirtation. And she saw in the comic-book girl exactly the sort of buxom, skull-accessorized minx that would prove a threat, if Terrence got close enough to get a good look at her.

Nina felt overdressed in her First Lady getup and would have gone so far as kicking off her shoes and unbuttoning something, when a side door opened. The man she recognized from the gallery Web site stopped in the doorway, letting the door hit him gently from behind.

"This is your three-thirty," said the minx.

"Oh," said Hank Gilliam in a mild voice, almost inaudibly. "You're Nina Whatsit?"

"I am," said Nina, offering up a smile she had practiced in the mirror, confident but not too willing to compromise—happy, but with that hint of maturity. This was quite a lot of nuance to pack into a smile, and Nina felt the smile's failure in the cunning, mordant gaze that met hers. She was about to say her name completely and correctly, but her effort was interrupted.

"Atwood," corrected the minx. "Nina Atwood."

Nina had always liked her name, and thought that it was compact and perky. Now her name sounded stiff and fake on the unfamiliar lips, and the minx got it wrong: *Nine-uh* Atwood, not *Neena*.

"Well, you better come on into the back," said Hank Gilliam.

She left Terrence leaning on the wall beside the receptionist, and she caught the words *Lucas* and *sound track*, a conversation that made Nina want to go out and grab Terrence by the arm and drag him along.

28

She followed the owner through a doorway into what looked like a dark, unnaturally shadowy chamber, illuminated, from the ceiling, by a single, arctic-blue beam of light.

The room was cold, the exhalation from the air-conditioning bearing down on the two of them.

"Let's see what you got," said Gilliam.

He was a short man with plenty of hair, combed back straight, and a beard that was trimmed down to stubble. He wore a black cashmere sweater, and dark pants with a bright silver buckle. In the half dark, half light he tended to vanish and reappear as he stepped forward and back. Nina did not like the man's low-key, side-of-the-mouth way of speaking, or the faint sexual implication behind what he had just said.

Her hands were colder than the room. She unzipped her portfolio and withdrew the picture Terrence and she had picked out to go first, the Bay Bridge at night, one of his favorites.

"Just spread the things out on the table," said Gilliam, "all at once."

The things.

She struggled with the canvas container, which fought her grip, buckling and slumping.

"Like this," he said.

He gave the portfolio a shake, and the pictures fanned out, expertly displayed like a grand deck of cards. The expensive professional-grade photo paper made soft sounds, like breathing. He tugged a pair of white gloves out of an inner pocket, and worked his fingers into them, flexing his hands.

She had to form a bond, however uncomfortable, with this gallery wizard, so she suggested that she call him Hank. "Is that all right?"

"Of course," he said.

Then he said nothing, setting forth the prints into the corners of the table, asking her technical questions about megapixels and dots per inch.

She answered his questions easily—she knew what she was doing with cameras and printers. He looked at the parking garages with his finger to his lips, he mused over the wet, rainy streets, and he pondered the fog-dusted off-ramp. Nina told herself that she should have cropped the bridge, and saturated the night shot of Geary Street, every photo looking suddenly unfinished.

"No people, I take it," he said.

She did not follow his meaning for a moment.

"You don't have pictures of people," he said.

"No," she said. "I don't do portraits very often."

"I don't mean faces," he said, examining her picture of low tide, blue rivulets down to the sunset-roiled water. "We live in the epoch of the dominating face," he added, "and I get really tired of eyes and smiles."

She began to think that maybe she and Hank Gilliam could agree on something, although she would have loved to take another picture of Terrence, or a new one of her brother.

"You need someone naked," he said.

She said, "I beg your pardon?"

"Nudes—collectors love them."

"I haven't worked with live models," said Nina.

"Or dead people," he offered in his small, alarmingly quiet voice. "Dead bodies don't sell, but they pull the collectors in."

"I don't feel like taking pictures of corpses," she said, feeling like a lady confronted by a gargoyle.

He searched through the prints, handling them carefully and slowly, making no comment for a long moment.

He asked, "How old are you?"

She told him her age, while feeling that he was probably weighing the legal penalties for statutory rape.

"You'll need a parent to ink the contract," he added.

"I don't understand," she said.

Then he said, "These pictures are fine."

She still did not understand. From her father, a word like *fine* meant adequate, *The coffee's fine*. The word did not mean much in the way of praise.

"Your photographs have style," he said.

More bleak praise, she thought.

"Do you like any of them at all?" she asked.

He said, "I'm thinking winter."

Then they were back in the exhibition room.

Gilliam spoke to the receptionist.

"Chelsea," he said, "print up a contract for Ms. Atwood."

Only when Nina saw Terrence's face light up did she let herself comprehend what was happening.

"Nina," Terrence said joyfully, "you did it!"

29

The same street that had looked like a jumble of humanity was now a serene setting of people enjoying the afternoon.

She and Terrence became two of these people, sitting outside Big Nuke Café and sharing a cranberry scone. She was jubilant.

"This might turn out to be," she said, "the happiest day of my life."

"You deserve it," said Terrence.

The platform of the Rockridge BART station was between the lanes of a freeway running east and west.

The traffic rushed past, trucks rumbling and smaller cars slashing by with a sound like wet breeze, and with the trains running slow because of an accident on the tracks in Hayward, there was time to read.

Nina was reading now.

She leafed through the many pages of the Gilliam Gallery artist/exhibitor contract, and what she read among the numbered and lettered sections of prose made her happiness begin to fade, and then as she reread she began to lose her joyful mood altogether.

"It says here that the photographer has to pay all material costs," she told Terrence. "And pay for the matting. I'll have to shell out for the glass and the frames, not to mention the photo paper and the printing expenses. The estimated outlay for an exhibit is six thousand dollars."

"How can you ever make any money?" asked Terrence.

"If I sell a picture, I get half the proceeds," she said, finding the paragraph with the percentage signs. She felt disconsolate, even when Terrence put his arm around her.

She pulled her phone out of her pocket, and when she heard Chelsea answer she said she had to speak to Hank right away.

Chelsea said that she would see if Mr. Gilliam was available. "But I believe that his appointments are fully booked for the rest of the day."

"I insist," said Nina.

Terrence took his arm away, as though not able to offer reassurance to a person this angry.

When she heard Hank's muttered greeting, she said, "There is no way that I'm going to be able to afford to put on a show."

"Well, I'm sorry to hear that," said Hank. "That's a real shame."

With the banging and sighing of the traffic she could hardly hear him.

"Of course," he added, "we could always work something out."

A huge truck went by, shaking the air. The sign above the platform indicated that their train would arrive in two minutes.

Nina asked, "Like what?"

30

After Terrence had left them, Milton and Bruce finished shoveling the dusty, rocky soil into the hole, and tamped the surface down with the backs of their shovels.

Milton thought they had done a good job. He felt happy and serene, the way he usually felt when something was satisfactorily finished.

But as he leaned the shovels in place in the toolshed beside the garage—the long, work-worn handles fitting in beside the hoe and the rake—Milton realized how absurd Bruce looked, his limbs shock-green. Milton recognized that he must look almost exactly the same.

The problem was highlighted in his mind when a neighborhood cat four-footed his way into the backyard from the half-wild expanse of the hill, wending through the blackberry vines and giving the two brothers a casual, feline glance.

Milton knew this cat well, and the neutered tom always

coiled his way between Milton's legs, or stopped by so Bruce could tickle his chin. But now the yellow, tiger-pattern cat stopped, one paw up. And stayed just like that for a long moment.

"Hey there, cat," said Bruce, in a friendly, inclusive way, the same way he would greet a human friend.

Bruce shared Milton's kind regard for cats and dogs and other animals. But on this day the cat was having none of it. His nostrils winked in and out, his eyes not bothering to look Bruce's way, or Milton's.

When he moved at last, he performed a quick beeline, under the collection of cement mixers, through the pink geraniums that thrived no matter how everyone neglected them, and then he was gone.

Even a cat could see they were not fit for companion-ship.

Milton had to get his hands on his father's skin-cleansing detergent, and to do that he would have to sneak into the house and get the keys to the basement.

This was not necessarily going to be easy.

He crept up the back steps and into the kitchen.

Mom was taking her post-lunch nap, but she actually rarely slept during this siesta. She kept the bedroom TV tuned to CNN and checked her voice mail, sitting up in bed and resting without actually falling asleep. Milton could hear the news now, a bright-sounding voice talking about an autopsy.

Milton tiptoed, snagged the basement key from its hook

by the mop and broom, and then lost no time getting back outside.

The key was old and the lock was worn, but at last the door opened. The basement was a crowded but well-ordered place of shadow and earthy, cool smell, the way Milton expected a cave would smell if the cave dwellers had claimed the place and started fixing it up but left it unfinished.

The space was murky but homey, with cans of vegetables and bottles of mountain spring water on wooden shelves. Mom had the idea that a major earthquake or a warlike disruption was more than likely at any time. She kept a reserve of canned foods and extra candles, and the items that only she would think of as necessary, like the packages of pastel-colored sponges and cheesecloth dishtowels folded and waiting, as though the primary task you want to perform in case of a nuclear war is to scrub the bathroom.

This was where the especially caustic cleaning materials were kept, too—the bleach and the stain remover—and this was also where the big jar of Dad's special cleanup goop was stored. Except that when Milton approached the place where the stuff was supposed to be, there by the big red box of snail poison, there was nothing. The shelf was empty, except for the unmistakable outline of an ebony hook and barb—a scorpion.

The scorpion was poised to attack, and Milton saw this not only as an extremely unpleasant threat—he saw it as a bad omen.

"Turn on the light," said Milton in a low voice.

Bruce stood at his side, but made no move to turn on the naked overhead bulb. Instead Bruce leaned forward, and to Milton's horror he picked up the offending arachnid between his thumb and forefinger and let the thing fall to the rough, unfinished floor.

"It's dead," said Bruce.

Milton considered what he had just seen—Bruce proving his better judgment, at least where a spiteful creature was concerned.

"Probably molted," said Milton.

One of his favorite Web sites featured scorpions and scorpion lore. He could not stand the creatures—but they fascinated him. "They shed their exoskeletons," he added, wanting to one-up his brother after being embarrassingly startled.

"I hate them, too," said Bruce, in a tone that was almost kind. He bent down and reached between the shelf and the obsolete clothes washer, and brought out a jar of amber-colored stuff.

He handed it to Milton. "That's what we need, isn't it?" he asked.

It certainly was. But Milton's mood of confidence was fading fast. He thought of the scorpion—where there was a cast-off skin, there was a living specimen nearby, bigger and full of life.

And he thought of Terrence, seemingly harmless and yet maybe not so inoffensive. You could not be too careful.

31

You probably misunderstood," said Terrence.

"What else do you think a man like Hank Gilliam means," said Nina, "when he says that we could 'take it out in trade'?"

Nina and Terrence had taken BART back to El Cerrito Plaza, riding in silence. The train had been crowded with people coming home from work, standing room only. Nina had been too hurt and upset to speak, and Terrence waited patiently for her to grow calm enough for discussion.

Now they were walking back up San Pablo Avenue. The late afternoon was cool here, in the long shadow of Albany Hill, low clouds skimming overhead. The cool wind was rising, Taco Bell wrappers spinning. Nina almost envied the hunched figures in the Hotsy Totsy Club, men and women safely out of the chilly breeze, drinking liquor in the light of big-screen golf.

Terrence was taking his time, aware that Nina was in a fragile mood. He said, "He doesn't necessarily mean sex."

You are so naïve, Terrence. She didn't say this, but the message carried in her silence.

"Well, maybe," admitted Terrence.

He had a way of backing up when confronted, but at the same time remaining gently determined, circling back to reassert his confidence. He showed this now when he added, "And maybe not."

"Listen, Terrence, there is a lot you don't know."

She began the assertion feeling annoyed, disturbed by what she knew was Terrence's dogged caution and good sense. But by the time she heard the words come out of her mouth, her annoyance was gone. Terrence had that effect on her—she couldn't stay angry.

But she could stay tough.

They continued to walk, past the pet hospital and the shop that sold trophies and plaques. The time Nina won the eighth-grade math prize, the framed tablet had been purchased here.

He said, at last, "Nina, I love you."

She couldn't argue with that.

Or the way she felt about him. She softened her voice.

"I got a look at Gilliam's password—Chelsea had it sitting there on her desk."

"You figured it out?" asked Terrence.

"It's pi to the right of the decimal, with a couple of variations," she said. "I could slip into the gallery and zap all his accounts to zero."

"Except you aren't a criminal," said Terrence.

"Maybe that way of looking at life," said Nina, "is obsolete. Maybe you have to do what you have to do."

"Is that what you think?" he asked.

Well, no, not really. She felt disillusioned, but not quite blasted beyond recognition. She had to say, however, "What I believe doesn't count for much."

Terrence was gentle, and squeamish about certain subjects, but she had to admit that he had a way of getting back to the main question.

"What does matter?" he asked.

"At any given moment," she said, "what matters is who has the money."

"Is that all that matters?" he responded, sounding mildly incredulous, but smart, too, knowing that he was right.

"Sometimes it's important," she said, "who has the gun."

Major Wanstead was working in his nasturtiums, judging from the indistinct shape silhouetted against the yellow house. He called out a greeting, and Nina took a moment to tell the veteran soldier that he had the best-looking garden in the neighborhood.

He thanked her.

"Sometime," added the major, "I'm going to take a few days and just sit and enjoy this place."

"Why not start today?" suggested Terrence.

"Tonight I'm off to Palo Alto," said the major. "I'm

chairing a meeting—recent war widows and widowers, what they can expect from their country now."

Not much, Terrence suspected.

"Will you be going after the owl tonight?" Nina asked Terrence when they had wished the major good luck with his presentation.

"Tonight's the night—Mom's excited about it."

"Let's hope the owl cooperates," she said. "Take your cell phone," she added. "Turn the ringer to vibrate so I don't scare off the owl."

They parted in a happy mood.

But as he ambled alone, up the walkway toward his front porch, he felt the nature of his handicap close around him. And he had increasing doubts about the Borchards. A family does not stay the same, season after season. They improve, they deteriorate, they grow wiser, or more violent.

That outline over near the pale hint of a mailbox might be a waiting assailant, and that shadow falling eastward from the house might hide anyone.

An attacker could be waiting, right there, beside the porch, thought Terrence.

And I would never know.

32

When she had parted from Terrence, Nina made a point of pausing briefly in front of Jocelyn Hurlow's two-story house.

The dwelling was white with blue trim, and the variety of bougainvillea vine that was so popular spread all over the side of Jocelyn's house, blowsy and unpruned, papery purple blossoms scattered like party trash.

Nina did not approach Jocelyn's front porch, but she did take a long moment to perceive Carraway's oxblood boots, neatly lined up beside the front door. Nina had been right about the new-carpet/no-shoes rule. The thump and resonance of music drifted out of the Hurlow home, and Nina had the impression that Carraway was being treated to Jocelyn's taste in country-and-western hits.

But the two shoes beside the woven tire-rubber welcome mat gave Nina hope that Carraway was not about to do anything rash. Surely that was the sound of Jocelyn's voice from inside the house, a pretty laugh, and Nina felt a stab of jealousy, this ordinary but good-looking woman captivating her brother with her bulk-import scents and French manicure.

But Carraway was entitled, she told herself, to a little romance after all that he had suffered. And maybe the welcoming embrace of the Bed Bath & Beyond employee of the month would keep Carraway from visiting the Borchards.

SHE STOPPED IN HER TRACKS as she approached her house.

A shaggy privet bush grew beside her front porch, a column of vegetation that had once been kept trimmed and neat by the gardener they could no longer afford. Mr. Santos had barbered the privet bush every other week with a hedge trimmer, the leaves and stems surrendering to his skill. These days the shrub was still pretty, but instead of a crisp outline it now gave the impression of untidiness.

Someone was waiting there in the cloud-muted, early evening light, sitting right where Terrence had been waiting earlier in the day.

This visitor spelled trouble. She knew it as soon as he made his first move, standing up and lifting a hand in greeting, going out of his way to look harmless and welcoming.

He came down the walkway, an individual she had never met before. He spoke her name, in a tone of calm inquiry, and she knew right then who he was.

"Sergeant Palmer," she said, holding out her hand and taking his, looking into his green eyes.

He was a rangy man her brother's age, with long arms and big hands. He was dressed in a civilian windbreaker and running shoes, but the clothes did not quite suit his bearing, a man used to wearing camouflage and a flak jacket.

She said, "Carraway's not here."

33

He didn't talk again right away, but waited until they were in the house, and Nina had turned on a floor lamp against the first evening darkness.

"I need to talk to him," said Jerry Palmer.

"Tell me," said Nina, "why my brother doesn't want me to mention your name?"

"Well, I didn't always have the same opinion about things as he did," said Jerry. He looked around at the living room, listening to the vacant rooms above him. "We actually had a disagreement now and then."

"About what?"

"Tactics." He let that answer sink in, and then he continued. "But I consider myself a loyal friend."

The wind made the house creak. Jerry glanced upward again.

"He's not here," she said. "I told you that. Why don't you sit down?"

"Do you know where he is?" he asked.

He's visiting on old girlfriend, she nearly said. But she felt protective of her brother, and sensed that Jerry was someone to keep away from.

"He had a girlfriend," said Jerry. "Jolene Something. Maybe he's visiting her," he added. "You could tell me her address—I have to talk to him right away."

"Jocelyn," she answered, and added, without a trace of truth, "I'm not sure where she lives."

"They've just ordered me back to Camp Roberts," he said.

The question popped right out of her, before she could stop it. "Was there some kind of problem?"

Jerry gave an aw-shucks smile, but she could see how he really felt. "Some kind of investigation," he said. "That's what I need to talk to Carraway about."

"You sound like you're from cattle country somewhere," she suggested, happy to change the subject, just as Carraway did so often. "Somewhere country-western, like Texas."

"Modesto, originally," he replied, naming a Central Valley community. "My folks had a spread of cattle east of there, but they recently bought a horse ranch in the wine country."

"So you're a Golden State cowboy," she said.

"You might say that."

People who called their parents *folks* always sounded agreeable to her, old-fashioned and polite. "We have some miso soup, Jerry, freeze-dried instant but not bad, and a couple of eggs, if you're hungry. And a half liter of pink grapefruit juice."

"I don't want to cause you any inconvenience," he said. "But I think that Carraway should know that the army has begun a murder investigation."

"Who was killed?" she asked, as though this was all news to her.

"Some bodies were found," he continued, "in the desert west of the Safwan refugee camp."

"Dead bodies," she said.

"Very dead bodies. Gunshot wound victims," he said.

"Carraway didn't do anything," she said.

She kept her voice steady, like she was sure of her facts.

She knew her brother would not hurt anyone without good cause. But the new Carraway, just back from the war, troubled her. She knew her brother was innocent—but she was not completely certain.

"That's what I hope we can get fully established," said Jerry.

"You want to talk to him so you can get your stories straight," she suggested, hating what she was saying. But there it was, her nagging doubt regarding Carraway. She couldn't entirely hide her feelings.

"We used to sit in the desert at night," Jerry continued, "Carraway and me, and watch the tanks go by. It's not a safe thing to do, because the tank drivers can't see very well and you could get run over easily in the dark. But Carraway loved the way the tanks come up through the night, with that *squeak-squeak-squeak* they make."

Nina didn't want to hear any more, but she could not keep herself from listening intently.

"One afternoon," he continued, "we arrested two suspects with backpacks full of Abrams tank parts—primary sights, auxiliary sights, hydraulic lines, turret control switches, all rifled from tanks that had been damaged and left while repair crews were choppered in. The crews arrive, but the rats have already been there, stripping the American armor down."

Jerry shook his head at the memory.

"We handcuffed the thieves, but we knew we'd have to let them go. Carraway volunteered to walk them back to the refugee camp, just to see that they were escorted where they couldn't turn around and steal more stuff. I was tired, and nobody else wanted to carry out the duty, but Carraway insisted."

"Are you saying," said Nina, "that Carraway was in charge of the suspects?"

Jerry did not answer right away. "You know how sure of himself Carraway is. How angry he gets."

Nina felt furious. Her brother was not a murderer.

Was he?

"I should tell you to get out of our house," she said. "Right now."

34

The problem isn't that Carraway is facing certain court-martial," Jerry continued, "or even that he might be caught and face military prison. The American authorities don't like to publicize crimes like this. Besides, the case against him is circumstantial, no witnesses, no ballistic evidence, the prisoners all shotgun victims. Bad things happen out in the desert."

"So you're reassuring me that even if my brother is a cold-blooded killer," she said, "he will almost certainly escape prosecution."

"Well, I wouldn't put the situation that way," said Jerry. "But yes. Even here in the Bay Area nearly half the murders go unsolved."

Nina considered for a moment. "But they are still murders."

"Yes, they are." Jerry let this affirmation hang in the air. Then he added, "And murder demands justice."

"Do you think Carraway did something to those prisoners?" she asked.

Jerry did not meet her eyes for a long moment, and then he did, looking right at her as he said, "Yes, I think he did."

"I have heard about enough from you," she said, "coming in here, slandering my brother." She started this statement with a strong voice, but ended in tears.

"My concern is," said Jerry, "that he is going to come back into civilian life, and keep acting the same way he did in Iraq."

"You mean, taking justice into his own hands." She pictured his hands as she said this, how he showed her how life had sheltered her.

"I think maybe I'd like a little of that grapefruit juice, after all," he said, "if it's not too much trouble."

He drank the juice down fast, and thanked her. His hands were trembling. She saw how difficult this had been for him, telling her all these bitter facts.

"Do you carry a handgun?" she asked.

"No," he replied, not looking all that surprised at the question. He sounded very much the cop when he added, "I'm not licensed to carry a concealed weapon off military property." Then he said, "I'm worried about Carraway, but I don't think I need an actual armored division to go after him."

"You hold yourself like someone who's carrying a gun. Like you have it on your belt there, behind your hip."

"Not me," he said.

"When he comes back, I'll tell him to call you."

"Don't bother," he said. "I'll see you again."

She saw him off toward his stone-white PT Cruiser, parked on the other side of the street, and as she watched him amble across the pavement she saw him put his hand to the back of his hip, the same half-conscious gesture Carraway had made. He was feeling for his weapon, making sure it was safe.

Jerry had lied about carrying a gun.

If he lied about that, she thought, what other lies was he telling?

35

Louella Borchard asked what Milton and Bruce had been up to that day as she ladled out their supper, spinach pasta and cheese sauce, with sliced purple onion salad.

"Not much," was Milton's response.

She gave him a look—her most suspicious glance—and went over to the sink for the salt and pepper shakers.

The jar of cleaning goop from the basement had worked its miracle, with a great deal of scrubbing, and now the two brothers were their customary color, although perhaps more pink than usual. The cleaning chemicals had a strong smell, and as Milton sat there he was aware of the odor of petroleum distillate coming off his limbs—the smell of toxins that could dissolve oil spills.

The kitchen floor gave slightly under Mom's feet—years of invisibly active termites had weakened the studs, along with the water damage from the time Dad fell asleep and the tub upstairs overflowed for hours.

Bruce shoveled in the food—he loved Mom's green noodles. He looked at Milton, giving him a glance that said, *Look, I'm still being quiet.*

"You both took long showers," she said, "and you scrubbed the shower stall after you were done."

Long showers were a family tradition, but cleaning up with a sponge and foaming cleanser afterward was not normal behavior for either brother.

"Just helping out with the housekeeping," said Milton, wondering what had made him think they could get away with bank robbery under Mom's nose.

"What was that car I saw you in?" she asked. "That old tan Taurus?"

Milton had expected her to notice the car, and he had rehearsed a decent answer to the question.

"The Ford, you mean," said Milton.

She said, "That's right."

She sat down, letting her weight settle in the bentwood chair, but she didn't look at either one of them for a while. She peered at the holes in the salt shaker, which tended to get clogged.

Milton remembered a few months back, when Mom had put on her white cashmere sweater and pleated pants to show up for his arraignment, after he had been arrested for being drunk on San Pablo Avenue.

In the courtroom she had looked pretty, in a way that had surprised him. Anxiety for her eldest son and a little extra mascara made her look lively and even stylish, and the judge must have liked what he set his eyes on. Milton had been released on his own recognizance, and no bail had been required. Now his mother had an entirely different appearance, slumped in her favorite chair in the pink bathrobe with her name stitched on the breast.

"The car was sage color," Milton said, hoping to distract her with details that did not really matter. "Light green. Bruce was adjusting the starter for someone."

"We made some money," said Bruce.

He looked at Milton for retroactive permission to say what he had just said, and Milton wished he could push a delete button and erase not only Bruce's speech but more than a good portion of his personality, maybe his entire existence.

Mom put her hand out, reached over, and gave Bruce's arm a pat.

She had hung art on the walls of the kitchen, French peasants harvesting shocks of hay, cute stone bridges spanning multicolored canals. The top of the refrigerator held boxes of jigsaw puzzles.

She had studied at Long Beach State University before she found out that what she really wanted to do was talk to longshoremen over a loudspeaker, announcing arriving freighters. She had worked at San Pedro Harbor and the Oakland waterfront, living an intermittently lucky existence until her husband had been killed and her lungs gave out.

"But we were here all morning," said Milton, his only 100 percent lie so far.

She took a rolled-up paper napkin from a Harrah's Reno highball glass and touched it to her lips.

She loved them both, Milton knew. But she thought him hard to figure out, while Bruce was her overgrown, misunderstood baby. Over the years, Milton had found her going through the books in his backpack, the history of flight and the biographies of assassins. But books about deep-sea diving, too, and the Civil War, not to mention submarines and martial arts. And poetry. Milton tried to stay well-rounded.

"We drove the car down the block," he said, amending his lie a little, "but otherwise we were around here all day."

She took the napkin from her lips, the paper stained faintly with lipstick.

She said, "I saw you digging."

Milton made an *I don't think so* expression.

"And I saw you talking to that Quinion kid, Terrence," she said, indicating with a toss of her head the kitchen window, where the four panes of glass had a view of the Borchard property, all the way to the poison oak of the hill.

"He's blind," said Milton, wishing that the same thing could be said for Mom.

"He's not that blind, and he records things," said Mom.

"That's right," said Bruce. "He's recording an owl up on the hill tonight."

Mom considered this, but for the moment she made no additional remark.

Milton was aware that he bore the same name as a great poet, John Milton, who had been vision-challenged. And Milton had long held a respect, and even awe, for the sight-less. The California State Orientation Center for the Blind was at the top of Adams Street not far from the Borchard home, and Milton was accustomed to seeing nearly blind people learning how to be even more blind. They wore black eyeless masks and tap-tapped along the sidewalks with their white sticks, a teacher in tow to keep them from walking out across busy San Pablo Avenue against the traf-fic lights.

But there was something deceitful and fraudulent about a guy like Terrence Quinion, who got sympathy for being practically legally blind, but who could probably see suffi-ciently well to identify Bruce and Milton to the police.

In fact, thought Milton, if there was ever an individual who deserved to be modestly but concisely killed to pre-vent him from spreading reports of what he might have more or less seen, and what he might have captured with his movie-quality bird and nature recording machine, it was Terrence Quinion.

Milton considered his next statement carefully.

"Maybe you shouldn't know what we did today," said Milton.

"Maybe I should," she said.

Mom was smart and dangerous. She had spent years overlooking the tardiness of her husband, a man who once drove the pickup all the way up the front steps, in a bout of drunkenness so profound it would have been comical if it had not been so hazardous. Bottles of sour mash secured in the geraniums, liters of vodka tucked away behind the half-inflated rubber dinghy—she had lived by ignoring a great deal.

But in recent years she was learning to survive, and she studied lengthy weekly e-mails from the pro bono lawyer and was planning an improved Web site dedicated to victims of corporate injustice. She maintained a blog that recounted her views on how governments ripped off their citizens—every government, everywhere. She had an illness that would probably kill her within a few years, and she did not seek a silent, stupid existence for herself, or long prison terms for her sons.

Milton had a vivid memory from the months just before his dad was killed in the explosion. He came upon Mom standing over her passed-out husband, holding a baseball bat in both hands, lifting the club, ready to bring it down on the drunkard's skull.

Maybe he had interrupted a murder, walking into this very kitchen for a Diet Dr Pepper. Milton knew all this now, and so he remained careful. The aluminum bat was still not far away, leaning beside the water heater.

Mom had mentioned the incident with the bat only once, a few days later. She had been paying bills, slipping checks into envelopes at the kitchen table. "I wouldn't hurt him, Milton," she had said. "Not in real life. But by God, if I did, no one would blame me."

A school psychologist once asked Milton what hardships had resulted from having a father who was an alcoholic. Milton had said there had been no particular hardship that he could think of. The psychologist would have been wiser if he had asked: What was it like to have a mother who did not really mind being a widow?

"Mom, let's say," Milton said now, "that theoretically we got involved in something complicated and messy today."

"What did you do?" she asked.

Well, there it was, thought Milton—the big question.

Bruce gave him a fleeting look, and then did not meet his eyes. Milton wished that he could find a brightly lit room somewhere far away, with clean tables and simple wooden chairs, a peaceful place. He wanted to be among amiable strangers, people checking their text messages and drinking beer.

"We had an idea," said Milton, "how to get our hands on some money."

"Something criminal," she said—not a question. She was looking right at him.

He considered his answer. "Strictly speaking," he said.

He was proud of that. *Strictly speaking,* like a diplomat.

"I heard helicopters, didn't I," she said, and this was not really a question, either. "And sirens."

"Did you?"

"I can hear, can't I?" she said.

This was when he had to take a risk. If Mom was going

to pick up the baseball bat and hit him, this was when she would do it.

Mom did him a favor—she shook her head and said, "Don't tell me any more. I can guess."

Milton kept his mouth shut.

"And it's my fault," she continued. "My fault, and your father's. And the refinery's fault, and the insurance company's fault. It's sugar's fault for being so unstable, tiny grains of the stuff in the air. A little static electricity and you have an explosion."

Milton did not like her to go on in this philosophical vein, not only because it was heavily weighted with self-pity and a generalized bitterness, but also because her mood at times like this could easily turn to real anger—if everything was everyone's fault, then Milton had to be to blame for something.

Still, her reaction could have been worse, and he felt lucky.

"It's not as bad as you think," said Milton.

He silenced Bruce with a glance—he had been about to open his mouth. *It's worse,* he had been about to say with a laugh. And Bruce would have been right to cut loose with a guffaw at that moment.

And then Mom aimed both barrels of her judgment right at Milton. "Maybe you're going to be one of those people who get into trouble, Milton, but you don't have to drag Bruce into it."

Bruce made a waving motion, back and forth with his hand, like a referee calling time-out.

"Don't blame Milton," said Bruce, and Milton felt a little stab of gratitude.

"I'll blame him, honey, if he gets you in jail," said Mom in her rarely used tender-voice, giving her younger son another pat.

Milton said, "We buried the evidence."

Mom screwed the cap on the ranch dressing very tight and then she shook the bottle up and down. She liked salad dressing on her purple onions—Milton preferred them bare.

Evidence, Milton knew, was a weighted word. You don't bury evidence unless there's guilt.

"Let's hope," she said, pouring out the dressing, "that you don't have to bury the witness."

36

Milton felt peaceful, but in a jittery, provisional way.

Pasta and cheese always made him feel good. He sat in the twilight after supper, drinking a can of Lo-Carb Monster. His weight was supported by one of the aluminum lawn chairs, a piece of furniture that his brother had repaired using vinyl sashes from a chaise longue someone had abandoned in the creek last year.

Shaggy, uncut grass rustled beneath his feet. He had buried his best Nikes with the ruined swag and the rest of the clothes, including Bruce's cherished leather jacket, and Milton wore his old, worn, and not-so-good Converse low-tops.

He had donned a Ben Davis pullover and a pair of Diesel roomy-fit jeans. He was full of Mom's cooking, and feeling relief that the day had gone as well as it had. He was peaceful, but it was the calm of alligators at the zoo, calm and even torpid, but inwardly aware. Inwardly aware of something—he was not sure how alligators felt.

He had searched for images of Bruce robbing the bank on the Web, but could not find any. Maybe, he thought, the KTVU news would feature their crime later that night, but perhaps, compared with murder and kidnapping, bank robberies were too commonplace to get much mention.

His mother was moving about the house, the dishwasher all loaded up, talking to one of her lawsuit friends on the phone. She sounded relatively contented, a homey vision in her pink bathrobe, padding around the kitchen saying, "I know, I know," in a tone of rapt compassion.

So Mom was so discontented with her life, it turned out, that the thought of her sons turning to serious crime did not deeply disturb her. Milton was a little surprised. But he was relieved, too. And her position made sense. This was not a courtly era, like the ones Milton had read about, with Robert E. Lee and Ulysses Grant agreeing like gentlemen to end the useless bloodshed.

Bruce had vanished up the ladder that he had brought from the garage, a rattling aluminum contraption he used when he got on the roof and repaired the flaking cedar shingles. Milton believed that Bruce probably smoked cigarettes up behind the eaves—his mother had threatened to choke him to death if she caught him lighting up.

Bruce was probably observing the vicinity from behind the retrofitted chimney while he coughed his way through a Marlboro. The old redbrick chimney had been taken down and replaced with a boxy, fireproof frame Bruce had built, nearly up to code, Milton was sure, but no one wanted a municipal building inspector around here.

After a while the aluminum ladder rattled and vibrated as Bruce made his way down from the roof.

He shook Milton's shoulder excitedly, although Milton was fully awake and in no need of being aroused.

"The major just drove away," said Bruce.

"OK," said Milton uncomprehendingly, not really following Bruce's thinking. Or perhaps he followed it, without really liking where he thought it might be leading.

"We can get into his house," said Bruce in an excited whisper, kneeling down on the wet grass. He wore a charcoal-gray zippered warm-up jacket and matching pants, and looked like a stylish track star.

"He probably just drove off to 7-Eleven for some milk," suggested Milton, feeling suddenly dismal, not for the first time that day.

"He was wearing a suit," said Bruce, spacing the words out, so that the point behind the words could not be missed. "A dark suit with a red necktie. He's going off to give one of his speeches."

They were all proud to have the major in the neighborhood, a man who said hello to everyone, regardless of age, race, or sex, and who gave interviews to the TV news about how every day should be Memorial Day.

"You're right, he might be going to do that," said Milton pensively, but with a stirring of excitement, too.

"You could watch the major's back door," said Bruce, "while I go in."

Milton squirmed in his chair, the hinges creaking. "You have to plan this sort of event," said Milton.

Event was a good word. *Traumatic event. Interstellar event.*

"We need a gun," said Bruce, as though that blunt fact canceled any other consideration.

"You can't just burst upon the scene," said Milton, standing up, feeling that bursting upon scenes was what his brother liked to do. "But we don't need a gun right this very minute, do we?"

Bruce said, "We're not done."

Milton had to admit that Bruce's character had momentum. He had force and he had audacity.

Bruce continued, "We might go for the Loomis car, right?"

The plan sounded better in his own head than it did coming out of Bruce's mouth. Milton said, "We might."

"And we have that witness problem Mom talked about," Bruce added.

Yes, that was a strange detail, thought Milton. She had made the remark out loud, and both of them had heard it. If you didn't know better you might believe that Mom was advocating killing Terrence. If not quite advocating the necessity, she had certainly put it right out there to be duly considered.

Milton said, "Yes, we do."

But he had his doubts. The intention to kill a person

was one thing. Finding a tasteful and even merciful way to commit the act was quite another matter.

"Then," said Bruce, "we better get a gun."

MILTON DRAGGED THE GARAGE DOOR OPEN—Bruce had left the door slightly ajar when he had extracted the ladder, and this annoyed Milton a little. He preferred to keep the place locked. The garage was a venerable wooden structure, with sliding doors and windows festooned with cobwebs and sun-dried husks of moths.

The Toyota pickup truck was stored here, under a coat of dust, but what was important about this place was that so much else was here, too—the fragments and fittings of a civilization. Here there were fresh batteries, and two small flashlights. Here were tools, a screwdriver, and an inexplicable number of gloves.

Milton was aware of the presence of his father, a man who kept a bottle of Bacardi on the workbench beside the spirit level and the sagging carton of roofing nails. Here, too, was the old Magnavox radio, spotted with paint, that had been the source of baseball and basketball play-by-play throughout Milton's boyhood.

If Terrence was going to be killed quietly, thought Milton, the best method would be a blow to the temple with a sack full of fishing weights. There was an entire drawer full of lead weights, and a skull-crunching weapon they would make, too. But an improvised weapon like that was crude and unpleasant.

"We'll each carry a flashlight," said Milton, as much to assert authority as to explain the obvious. He needed more time to think.

Bruce's flashlight worked, and so did Milton's, the beams shooting around at fishing nets and hacksaws.

The garage was a repository of a square-built masculinity. An old Half and Half pipe tobacco can held two or three pounds of Phillips screws. An ax hung on the wall, in brackets Milton could remember his father gluing together, when Bruce was still in diapers and Milton himself was so young he was afraid of the cactus that grew out beyond the house, sure that the plant harbored a monster.

The sight of the ax moved Milton to come to the decision that a firearm was the civilized and right-thinking way to proceed. If Terrence was going to be killed, he needed to be dispatched quickly and even mercifully. It was not proper for Bruce and Milton to stalk around the hill with an ax or a makeshift truncheon.

Milton took his time.

He was edging toward a plan that he held as plausible necessity. He felt no malice for anyone, and he was not considering acting out of anger, or petty vengeance. He was not sad or resigned, either. He felt keen, while retaining the usual mental habits of caution and circumspection. The plan was still in its sketchy stages, but the intention was clear, and could be carried out that very night.

He was planning murder, in the first degree.

37

Nina peered out from behind the front window curtains and watched Jerry Palmer's PT Cruiser disappear up the block.

She waited a long while, letting the unsettling feeling of the man's presence leave the room.

Nina did not believe in ghosts, and she had no sense of afterlife. But she kept her mother's spring-yellow blouse in her bedroom closet for more than reasons of unfinished bereavement, or simple sentiment.

Something, Nina believed, endures. And what would this remnant guardian, this absent smile, her mother's lingering faith in her, advise now? She went into her bedroom and took the blouse from the place where she kept it safe at one end beyond the usual clothing, on an old wooden hanger.

Sometimes she thought she could still smell her mother in the fabric. She loved the mother-of-pearl buttons, and the way the buttons were not one color, but all the colors, every hue, all at the same moment.

"Mother," she asked aloud, in a low voice. "What would you tell me?"

Only you.

SHE HURRIED UP THE STREET, not letting herself think what she kept trying to think, keeping a grip on herself. She knew that she would find her brother safe and happy in Jocelyn's house, and yet she did not know it for sure.

She felt very uneasy.

So when she paused outside Jocelyn's pretty bungalow-style house and saw Carraway's ankle-high boots still lined up there, toes against the wall, she was relieved.

Nina knocked on Jocelyn Hurlow's door.

In the past, Nina had been aware that knocking on a door, and pressing the use-smudged button of a doorbell, was a source of minor anxiety. She had known that life was filled with sources of suspense. But she had never been so acutely aware of the length of time a human being needs to get up from whatever romantic, reclining position she had adopted and walk slowly across the new living room carpet.

Music was playing, not the country-and-western bass twangs of earlier in the day, but the kind of mood-sustaining music you leave on for hours, watered-down compositions, light classical fare. She heard this music diminish into near-silence as the steps paused beside the source of the sound, and then the footsteps continued their approach toward the doorway.

THE DOOR OPENED.

Jocelyn Hurlow was quite pretty.

Nina had not actually looked right into the woman's face for a long time, and now, with Jocelyn's hair every which way, and a light robe fastened around her body, Nina felt her usual dislike for the woman temporarily vanish.

Nina was glad she was still wearing her killer interview outfit, with a leather warm-up jacket against the chill. Her ensemble was certainly better thought through than Jocelyn's lavender wraparound and her ballet slippers. Nina was glad, too, that she had put on a pair of running shoes, the yellow Reeboks—her sensible flats had hurt her feet.

"I need to speak with Carraway," Nina said.

"Oh, Carraway," said Jocelyn, putting her hand over her heart. "That man has been through so much!"

Nina was inside the house with a quick move, not quite invited in, but Jocelyn made no protest.

Everything here was fresh out of the box. Plump rose-colored satin pillows were parked on a white sofa, and the walls had been painted a face-slap pink, with blue accents perched here and there, a cobalt-blue glass vase with a blue silk iris, a plush blue throw rug, the blue crystal statuette of a deer.

The new white carpet extended all over, into every corner, down the hall. The place smelled new, an odor that was bracing and fake. She felt that the smell in the air could not be healthy, and she called for Carraway, her voice caught and muted by the new carpet that stopped right at the kitchen floor. *Come out of this chemically scented showroom,* she wanted to cry.

"He's not here now," Jocelyn was saying.

"He has to be here," Nina insisted.

She pointed out that Carraway's shoes, the half boots, were waiting on the front porch.

"He was here," said Jocelyn, "a little earlier in the evening, and the poor, dear man was so tired, after all the troubles he's seen."

Nina's dislike for Jocelyn began to return.

She let the woman take a moment to silently express her conquest with a smile—how the man of war had taken his rest on a bed here in this pink-and-blue employee-discount environment. But there was an insinuation behind what Jocelyn was saying—that a really kind and sympathetic sister would not have let her brother go visiting all over town, and maybe not let him go off to war.

"He took a long nap," added Jocelyn, "and then he found his other shoes."

"His other shoes?" Nina heard her voice inquire.

"His black Prada sneakers," said Jocelyn with a coy smile, her romantic triumph complete. "They were a gift from me, you know. He left them here during his last leave, months and months ago, and I kept them safe."

"Where did he go?"

"He said he could walk more quietly in the sneakers, actually *sneak*," she said. "And I think he said they would bring him luck."

"Where?"

"Oh, you know Carraway and his secrets," said Jocelyn.

"Did he give you a hint?" asked Nina.

Jocelyn was aware by now that some matter of urgency was electrifying Nina, but this insight made Jocelyn sound all the more vague.

"Something," said Jocelyn, "about investigating something."

Nina was out the front door, hurrying into the darkness in the direction of the Borchard property, but she could hear Jocelyn call out, "I think he was going to investigate a robbery."

38

Milton and Bruce walked along the street, in the direction of the major's house.

Milton felt that his own harmless-looking style of walking was superior to his brother's version, which looked potentially menacing no matter how Bruce tried to mute his natural physicality.

The twilight was richer now, an added glow from above as drifting overcast reflected the source of light. Bruce's white T-shirt looked salmon-pink and his teeth when he smiled looked reddish, an unsettling sight, but the uncanny lighting was fading fast.

"I'm going to feel a lot better," he said, "with a real gun."

Milton noticed a pang of affection in his heart for Bruce, a guy who liked straight-ahead simplicity. What Milton had in mind was that, whatever happened, Bruce would always carry the replica. Milton would keep the real gun.

The sidewalks and streets were almost entirely empty; a kid in the distance skidding along on a skateboard, an exhausted-looking man climbing out of a Volvo, home from some mind-paralyzing job. The two brothers took a long walk, past the bowling alley, and let the evening get totally dark.

With nightfall upon them, ambient light filling out the dim details, Milton and his brother approached the yellow house.

The major had a perfect lawn—perfect except for a blond patch where a dog had apparently peed a healthy quantity. The only type of flower in Major Wanstead's garden was the glorious nasturtium, and Milton approved of that robust, far-spreading flower, which extended to every corner. You could not see any of this very well—the city of Albany had switched to an energy-saving faint yellow streetlight in recent months.

Without any warning, Bruce ducked along the side of the house, where a neighbor's overhanging bougainvillea vine reached out and snatched at his clothing. One moment he was standing still, and the next he was on his way—typical Bruce. Milton followed.

The neighbor's luxuriant trellis spilled over onto the major's property, and Milton was thankful. They waited in the inky shadow under the vine. Milton made himself as invisible as he could, fitting into the darkness, and he listened for any sign that they had been seen.

He clung to Bruce's arm—the one Mom had given an affectionate pat earlier that evening—and silently urged, *Wait.*

But Milton believed, reluctantly, that fortune favored the bold, so when Bruce hopped over the back gate, Milton followed, with a little more difficulty. Bruce crouched beside the green concrete patio, and put on a pair of gardening gloves, heavy-duty coverings stained with ancient chlorophyll and weed killer.

Major Wanstead's poorly lit backyard in no way resembled the Borchards' cluttered property. While Milton admired this verdant neatness, with the single, pristine birdbath dead-center, he also resented it.

What sort of stifling diligence required a man to pull all the little dandelions and clover flowers out of his lawn? The major had built a dinky green plastic roof over the place where the recycling and the trash were safe and snug. So much trimming and raking could be admired only if you didn't think of the hours of effort involved, and the arrogance—that the Wanstead real estate had to be the best-looking on the street. Even the parts that were not visible to the public.

Major Wanstead looked like everybody's uncle, asking how things were going with a smile, but Milton saw now that he was a repressive, doggedly organized man who deserved and required a robbery, just to restore the balance between his life and the mess of the rest of the world.

Milton was not pleased to see that Bruce was already forging ahead, stabbing the glass out of a kitchen window. He used his heavily gloved fist, working with a carpenter's carefulness. He snapped off fragments and set the triangles of glass on the close-cropped back lawn, where they began to look like the sort of puzzle Mom liked to work on, scenes of a seacoast or a foreign marketplace, portioned together to look like the illustration on the box lid.

That pastime had often struck Milton as pointless. Why put together a picture, fragment by fragment, when you already know the outcome?

But now he saw the wisdom of sitting around in your bathrobe, assembling the familiar poetry of famous paintings. That made a lot more sense than what he and Bruce were doing, further testing their luck by breaking and entering on a day during which they had already seen thousands of dollars blow up.

"If the gun has a lock," said Milton in a low voice, "don't forget to look for the key."

"I won't."

Bruce was all business now, getting the hang of this felony trade, and keen to show himself to be master of the enterprise.

"And don't get a gun," cautioned Milton, "that looks too hard to use." He had in mind the weapons he had seen in war movies, belts of ammunition, awkward tripods, adjustable gun sights.

"No problem."

Or too hard to conceal, he wanted to advise, *and don't get a gun without the right bullets.*

An entire chapter of advice nearly poured out of Milton, but he kept quiet as Bruce hoisted his body up and into the Wanstead home, and vanished into the interior.

39

Milton waited a long time.

The sprinkler came on in the backyard adjacent to Major Wanstead's garden, behind a fence, and a cool mist reached out and lingered over Milton.

Something moved.

A shape waddled out from a shrub-darkened cleft in the barrier. At first Milton thought this was a pudgy tomcat, or a raccoon, but he eventually made out the pale, tentative snout of a creature too ungainly to be anything but an opossum.

The creature lifted his snout, waddled forward, and peered at Milton.

Then it hurried along into the shadows, a graceless, almost uncanny visitation. Milton felt slightly offended. Sharing a space with an animal as lowly and peculiar as an opossum was a good enough reason to follow his brother into the house. He was concerned, too, at the lack of reports from inside, not even a call to his cell phone in case Bruce was stuck somewhere, or had trouble unlocking a gun case.

Besides, Milton was curious, never having been inside the major's house before. He put his hand on the window-sill, and the rest was easy. He boosted his body up and into a room with a washing machine and a dryer, the pleasant odor of soap and fabric softener soothing his anxiety.

He heard a distant footstep and followed the sound, his eyes catching hints of kitchen appliances and the wide expanse of a dining room table. He flicked on the flash-light briefly, but there were enough side lamps left on—in disregard of electrical rates, not to mention carbon emissions—to illuminate the rooms.

He called his brother's name in a loud whisper, and he heard the hint of an answering call. He followed the sound, but the walls seemed to take a step backward, and continued to shrink away from his touch as he proceeded.

The timbers and joists of the dwelling creaked all but silently, and Milton tensed. Surely that creak was the major coming home early. And that other scraping noise, over in a dark passage in the house, was surely a cop, sneaking closer, ready to do what cops did best—cuff Milton and his brother, and put them both into a jail cell.

This was a house of extreme, cruel tidiness. A flat, low-napped gray carpet extended down a hall, and in the rooms he passed Milton had glimpses of beds neatly made, and one chamber that was given over entirely to books.

All the volumes were in order, paperbacks on the lower

shelves, hardbacks on the upper shelves, with a picture of a city, with spires and a cathedral, on one wall. The rooms were small, but ready to be rioted in, as far as Milton was concerned—he had never seen a place of such airless, static order. A letter opener was laid out straight, parallel to the edge of the desk, with not a single other item on the desk-top.

Above the desk was a gun case, a cherrywood box with a glass door, displaying rifles and shotguns lined up, barrels pointed skyward. The glass was unbroken, the lock unmarred, and Milton left the case alone, hissing to get his brother's attention.

He found Bruce crouching beside a bed, the nightstand open and an automatic in his lap. At first Milton was sure that this was not a new possession at all, but the old novelty lighter. But Bruce let a handful of bullets flow from his palm, like treasure, and the bullets pattered heavily on the carpet, an authoritative percussion, like distant fireworks.

The sight of this firearm was astonishing, and even funny, in a way that made Milton not want to smile so much as to consider. The new pistol was the identical twin of the cigarette-lighter handgun that Bruce had been carrying, and in fact Bruce was pulling the cigarette lighter out of his waistband and brandishing it, his mouth open in a silent laugh.

"Give it to me," said Milton, and he wrapped his hand around the real gun. He gave a silent laugh, too.

He had a moment of inner quietude, and in this instant

of reverie he felt that he and Bruce would not have to kill Terrence Quinion.

They would simply go to the guy's house in a day or two and encounter him again, and really frighten him about keeping quiet. They would fall short of actual violence, very well short of consummating a murder, in the same spirit in which they had returned the stolen Taurus to the house on Key Route Boulevard.

But then Milton recollected that they had not actually returned the car to its owner, but had merely talked about doing such a decent, gracious thing. Their intentions had been quite separate from their actual deed, and in this case Milton also felt the grace fade from his heart, and a fresh determination take its place.

Milton gathered the bullets into his hand.

"It's already loaded," said Bruce. "Those bullets are extra."

Milton took the cigarette lighter pistol into his other hand. He put the pistols into the waistband of his pants, pulling his belt tight and buckling it again to make sure they were not going to fall down one pant leg or the other. The guns were heavy.

"Do you think we should set the place on fire?" asked Bruce.

Milton recoiled. "No!"

Although a certain justice would have been served, Milton realized, in cracking open this stiffly maintained, starched, and lifeless domicile.

"No," reasoned Milton, "we have enough to accomplish for one night."

An enlightened person like Milton did not despoil a house for no reason, not with his soul kindled and beaming, a source of destruction.

40

Nina ran.

As she hastened past the sleepy homes, bedroom windows alight, TV shadows flickering, she was aware how few people she actually knew along this street, and along any of the other avenues.

If she pounded on any of these doors for help, what would she say? And if she called the police, what crime would she report?

Nina could see why she loved taking photos of houses and streetlights, driveways and parked cars. Everything people set forth—every stepping-stone, every garage door —was alive with human presence.

A triangular sign with red reflectors indicated the street's dead end, and a white metal barrier kept cars from driving off into the wild flora of the creek. Nina had never actually approached the Borchard property before, except on Halloween, but everyone knew the place by reputation. The residence itself was a rambling white structure in the poor light, with a front porch crammed with cardboard boxes and newspapers as far as she could make out, all waiting to be recycled.

She skirted the house and hurried up the driveway, her running shoes crunching pea gravel. She worked the latch on a swinging gate and entered the backyard.

The place was a jumble of objects in the dark—boat hulls and lumber. She stumbled on a half-deflated rubber dinghy. The Borchards had always been building something, judging from deliveries of plywood and sacks of concrete over the years, but Nina had not realized the extent of their industriousness. Society might falter, but the Borchards would have a row of rusting cement mixers and several weed-pocked mounds of sand.

She saw her brother at the far end of the property.

A lightbulb fixed to the edge of a building sent a ray of illumination down to where her brother was standing up to his waist in a pit. A pile of dark earth was beside him, and a shovel was plunged into the soil, the shaft straight up.

Carraway leaned over and tugged at something, and brought forth a black plastic sack. He set the bag on the lawn. All the while he did this he was talking, speaking in a calm voice to a woman Nina recognized as Louella Borchard.

Louella was holding a baseball bat, gripping the thing like a weapon, holding it cocked like a batting champion. One more step, and she would be close enough to bring the bludgeon down on Carraway.

Carraway smiled as Nina approached, showing no great anxiety.

"Nina," he said in a tone of breathy triumph, "I found the money!"

"You're trespassing," said Louella. "Both of you."

She gave Nina a glance as she said this, but Nina sensed that Louella's mood was unsteady, and that, in her present emotional state, she was glad to see another woman.

Louella was wearing a patchy, rose-colored chenille bathrobe, as nearly as Nina could make out in the half-light, open to expose a Pyramid Ale T-shirt and a pair of dark sweatpants.

"You remember Carraway," said Nina, in a tone of neighborly brightness. "He's back from the war, just got here today."

"I read all about you," said Louella, almost lowering the bat. But then she adjusted her grip, keeping the metal shaft high over her head. "You are set to get a Bronze Star."

"That's right," said Carraway, leaning on the edge of the pit, not climbing out, happy to stay where he was. "For nearly being killed."

"The Veteran's Administration will rip you off," said Louella. "You want to speak to my lawyer."

Her baseball bat slowly descended, in gentle acknowledgment that she could not very well crack a war hero's head.

"Where are your sons?" asked Nina.

41

The brothers were careful to leave the house as undisturbed as possible, even straightening the wrinkles out of the long gray carpet in the hall. Their effort was selfless, even respectful. Having taken Major Wanstead's possessions in their hands, Milton had resolved that the veteran military officer deserved to find his domestic order almost entirely as he had left it.

"How will we do it?" Bruce was asking.

Milton did not like to enunciate his plans. He preferred to conceive, brood, and give orders, and this was no exception. Milton had a plan he did not want to explain to Bruce: Milton would do the killing—he did not want his brother to commit murder.

"Maybe we could just walk right up to the front door," added Bruce. "Point and shoot."

Milton felt a familiar frisson of exasperation, an almost pleasurable reminder that Bruce would never be the manager of a complicated undertaking. He didn't want his brother to kill anyone, but at the same time he could see the point of picking up a club and knocking his brother on the head until he permanently stopped saying stupid things. "We are talking about Terrence Quinion, right?"

Bruce walked along beside him, his arms close to his body, the cold bothering him. "That's right."

"Terrence Quinion is on the hill tonight," said Milton. "Recording the great horned owl. You know that." He stepped out into the middle of the quiet street and pointed. "Look there—you can see the flashlight."

A dim flare of illumination wandered upward, through the eucalyptus, toward the crest of the hill. The trees were visibly present even when you could not see them clearly, towering outgrowths that took on the ambient glow of city lights from the clouds.

"There are blackberry thorns up there," said Bruce moodily. "And poison oak."

"We have our own flashlights," said Milton. "And we know the trails."

Bruce began walking again, and the way he obediently made his way back in the direction of home and Albany Hill was his way of accepting Milton's guidance.

But Bruce's arguments were not finished. "He'll hear us coming. We should wait and take him when he comes home."

The cool night air made Milton walk all the faster, and he had to hurry anyway, to keep up with his younger, taller brother's long strides.

"We'll find him on the hill," said Milton.

"OK," said Bruce, and the way he said this, agreeing without really agreeing, bothered Milton. "But he's not alone," said Bruce, looking back so his words would carry. "I can tell by the way the light moves. Someone is helping him."

What did *that* mean, thought Milton.

"Nina's with him," Bruce was saying, "or his mom."

Milton knew that Bruce had to be wrong. Because if you climbed up a path on Albany Hill and killed not just a witness but also a girlfriend or a mother, that would be worse than a single murder.

But you had to see the logic, thought Milton, of taking the life of a witness. If you killed a human being because he could connect you to a robbery, you certainly had to kill a person who had seen you kill a human being.

"We'll go up the other side of the hill," said Milton, "and surprise them."

42

Where are your sons?" Nina repeated to Louella Borchard.

She needed to know, not simply to spare herself an unpleasant surprise. She was not sure what violence Carraway had in mind.

Louella set the head of the bat on the lawn and leaned on the implement like a makeshift crutch.

"I would be happier knowing," added Nina, "that they are somewhere safely far from here."

"You poor things," said Louella, ignoring Nina's query. "You and your family have been through hell, with the war."

"But it's going to be all right," said Nina with a tone of optimism that was entirely put on. "If we just know where Milton and Bruce are, so we don't expect them to suddenly appear."

"But things do suddenly appear," said Louella. "You can't see into the future."

"No, you can't," said Nina.

"One day you have a husband and two growing sons," said Louella, "and the next day a corporate lawyer is talking about blood alcohol and personal negligence."

"If the police found this money," said Nina, "you'd be talking to a defense lawyer about armed robbery. Carraway can take the evidence away, and burn it."

"You're not going to do that," said Louella, her voice not angry so much as weighted with lucid melancholy. "You want to pick up the reward from the bank."

"We have so much to talk about," said Nina.

"Like what, dear?" asked Louella.

This trace of tenderness surprised Nina.

"What am I going to do?" continued the weary woman. "I can't kill you and bury you here beside the garage, can I?"

"Why would you even consider such a thing?" asked Nina.

The woman lifted the baseball bat, but only to settle it more securely in the lawn. "To kill another couple of witnesses," she said, with an air of long-suffering sadness.

These words lingered in the air.

Nina heard them and then took a moment to mentally perceive them, gauging their meaning.

She was deeply troubled.

"Nina," said Carraway, "do you know where Terrence is?"

"He's on the hill," Nina responded, her voice thin with

emotion. "Recording the night birds, with his mother."

"With his mother?" queried Louella, sounding startled.

"Where are Bruce and Milton?" asked Nina, desperate for the answer.

"I'm worried," said Louella, "that they may be about to do harm."

Nina realized that a family who collected bathtubs and airplane wings, and held on to them, was a family that did not want to eliminate any options. If you got rid of a warped door, or recycled a crate of empty paint cans, you eliminated a possibility, however uncertain, and made your future that much narrower.

Such a family might well keep murder as an option, too—not as a definite plan, but as a possibility that could not be completely abolished.

Nina moved quickly.

She went over to the hole in the scruffy, water-starved lawn, reached down into the pit, and pulled the Beretta from her brother's holster—before he could protest.

Louella moved fast, too, the woman's shadow huge in the beam of light. She hefted the bat, lifted it high, the shadow of the club bending and folding over the obstructing undergrowth.

Carraway was out of the pit, climbing fast and gasping with the effort. Nina could see his shadow grappling with Louella's distorted, light-eclipsing shape. He took the bat away from her, judging by the shifting shadows, but Nina did not bother to glance back.

The automatic was heavy, and she held on to it tightly as she scrambled up the ramshackle fence, fighting to get clear of the blackberries and poison oak.

A fencepost held up, swaying and creaking, but at last the old wood gave way. A hidden spiral of barbed wire snagged her leg, tearing her skin, and she ripped her skirt.

She fought her way through.

43

Terrence had made a thermos of cocoa, his own recipe.

His mother could make hot chocolate, too, but his was better—Atwood Premium Imported Cocoa, the brand with Nina's father smiling on the label. You add a little cinnamon, a little salt, not too much Equal. You put it in the blender with hot water and fat-free milk.

Now the sound of the thermos top being unscrewed made a enormous, surreal sound in Terrence's earphones, like the top of a skyscraper being twisted off. The sound of the cocoa was amazing, too, a rush of fluid and then a gradually ascending tone as the liquid filled up the plastic cup.

His mother nudged him and handed him the container of cocoa, and he took a sip of the hot beverage.

The drink tasted good, and smelled good, too, but Terrence wondered what the scent smelled like to the night birds around him. Did the chocolate offend, with its lingering bittersweetness, or was the fragrance just another anomalous odor they associated with humans?

The great bird was overhead, on a protruding branch of a giant eucalyptus. The hunting fowl was so large, and his under-plumage so pale, that Terrence was almost convinced that he himself had caught a hinted glimpse of the wingspan overhead. This meant that the owl was aware of them, too, and as a result the hunting bird kept quiet.

The owl's voice made no sound. But Terrence was getting some other impressive sounds in his recorder, the *shush-shush* of the owl's wings, and the dry embrace of talons around the spindle of the branch. The owl stroked his beak on the wood, like a blade against a leather strop.

The owl yawned and gave his feathers a flourish, a noise like a dozen blankets shaken out. Feces emerged from the owl's gut, and pattered onto the dry leaves on the ground nearby, a report like a watermelon exploding onto pavement.

Terrence could feel the owl's eyes take in the landscape, the owl's vision so keen, Terrence had heard, that a single lighted match in a blacked-out stadium would allow the hunting creature to locate and kill a mouse. He could almost perceive the huge eyes as they blinked, and nearly sense the bird's vision drink in the landscape.

The night was a fabric of background murmur. A Union Pacific freight train grumbled past, drawn by two diesel locomotives, and the freeway made a continuous whisper and groan. But these sounds were easy to filter and mute, as he sat there adjusting his awareness of the planet.

Terrence thought he could hear conversation in the apartment beyond the hill, laughter, a wordless question. He liked these distant sounds, aware how much the living enjoyed being alive.

He could hear even more now. Another passing aircraft and a deep-throated diesel, a trucker gearing down somewhere far to the north.

He could hear much more than airplanes and trucks—he could even distinguish footsteps.

He adjusted his earphones.

He heard footsteps—no question.

He held his breath, listening with intensity. Clothing rustled, but these two people were as silent as a pair of hunters. They crept, and halted. They whispered.

And then Terrence continued to listen, but with slowly dawning dismay.

The desiccated, brittle eucalyptus leaves broke and crumbled, earth sighing under the shoes of two people. The dust was thick on some of the paths and this soft powder absorbed much of the noise the footfalls made. But the obdurate, jagged stones were giveaways, noisy despite the fact that these two people were approaching with care.

They advanced with exaggerated caution, pausing, feeling their way ahead, trying to use stealth.

Terrence heard whispers, and an answering voice, an indistinct remark.

Two familiar voices, still far off.

"No, I'll keep them both," said the same tense voice.

Terrence slipped off the earphones.

He tried to doubt the evidence of his ears, but he knew that would be foolish.

"Someone's coming, up the hill from the west," he said in a low voice. "Two people."

"Anyone we know?" asked Annette.

"I'm afraid so," he said.

"Who is it? Terrence, tell me who it is!"

His phone gave a high-pitched vibration.

Nina was calling.

"I'm phoning the cops," she said, sounding breathless and intense, "but you know how slow they are these days."

"What's wrong?" he asked.

"Milton and Bruce Borchard are on the hill, looking for you." She added, "I think they want to kill you."

44

The low clouds cast a weird, decay-colored light, enough to see by but not to make out anything in clear detail.

"Is there some reason," Bruce asked, "that you don't think I'm trustworthy?"

He spoke like this on purpose, using words he knew Milton had to respect. Bruce had never read a book, but he had heard Milton describe ancient battles, warriors giving their word.

"I think you are trustworthy enough," said Milton. He gave *enough* a certain slant as he spoke.

Bruce required more patience than Milton possessed just then. He could easily imagine sneaking a ride on the train passing along the edge of the bay, riding the rails down through Oakland and San Jose. "This isn't a good time to talk," added Milton.

"What do you think goes on inside my head?" asked Bruce.

Milton considered. "Pictures of you doing things."

"Like what?"

"Having sex," replied Milton. "Fighting, stealing things."

That shut Bruce up, Milton knew, because it was accurate.

They circled around through narrow streets crammed with parked cars, and began to hike up the opposite side of the hill. The dimly lit eucalyptus trees, with their tattered bark and scraggly limbs, reached upward, all around.

Bruce had a way of keeping quiet, but storing up what he was going to say, getting the words ready.

"I'm trustworthy enough to rob a bank with a cigarette lighter," Bruce said after a long moment, "but not with a real gun."

Milton truly and with all his heart did not want to have this conversation right then. But people developed, grew up, and maybe Bruce was starting to change. Maybe Bruce was maturing into a credible human being. That wasn't such good news—it made him all the harder to predict.

"We went into the bank," said Milton, "with the weapons we had."

"I went in," corrected Bruce. "Me."

He snapped on his flashlight and looked up at the trees, guiding the beam along the scarlet foliage of poison oak, picking out the trail. Bare branches stretched out, clinging to their legs.

"Turn out the light," said Milton.

Bruce complied. But just an instant of illumination changed the immediate vicinity. Roots spread out across the path, and the eucalyptus seeds were like small bell-shaped candies all over the trail, easy to slip on. Shadows welled and shifted, and clawlike plants reached out into the pathway.

"The way you use the flashlight is not responsible, just for example," said Milton. "Anyone could see us coming."

"I shielded the light with my body," said Bruce.

This was not true—Milton had seen the beam of light searching upward, into high branches.

"Walking down Solano Avenue with Billyana was not responsible, as another example," said Milton. He felt foolish bringing up the subject, but there—he had said it, the nagging episode that was on his mind night and day.

Bruce thought for a little while, maybe enjoying the memory. "Yes, well, she saw me outside Max's Liquors, and she stuck herself onto me."

"I'm sure everyone told her dad, and how pleasant do you think that was for her?" This was a very bad time to have this argument, but Milton could not just let Bruce walk around unchallenged. What did a beautiful young woman like Billyana see in Bruce, anyway?

"Let me carry the gun," said Bruce, lowering his voice to a whisper.

Milton felt his brother's superior size, aware that Bruce was strong enough to take the gun away if he wanted to.

"It's a matter of trust," said Bruce. "Prove you have faith in me."

"No, I'll keep them both," said Milton. His voice was a

little powerless. Bruce did not even try to argue in former times, except to register a complaint, or to badger Milton that it was time to go. *Prove you have faith* was an attempt at persuasion, a form of rhetoric.

Bruce put a hand on Milton, not an act of violence, but the hint of what might come, stopping Milton, as a parent might halt a child.

Bruce's grip was strong.

BRUCE KNEW WHAT MILTON HAD IN MIND, and he realized that his brother had a certain nobility of character. Milton did not want his younger brother to bloody his hands with murder.

But behind this position was plain arrogance. Bruce could not speak with enough eloquence to explain the ethics of his situation, but he had a deep sense of propriety, and he also knew when he was being slighted.

Milton believed that Bruce was inferior, not only in age, and not only in experience, but basically bred-in-the-bone substandard. Milton could think and talk, and Bruce could not.

Bruce was about ready to prove Milton wrong. On this night, Bruce would discover how much he could do, and Milton would be the astonished witness.

45

Milton was aware that Bruce was different tonight, no longer the simple second-in-command. However, Milton felt that in giving Bruce the replica gun, he might buy a few seconds.

Bruce would work the mechanism, try to cock the device, and realize that he had been tricked. He might even see the humor of this, and they could share a laugh. But the trouble was that Milton did not remember which gun was which, and he felt that either of the two automatics thrust into his waistband might be the weapon.

"We don't have time for this," Milton whispered. "We're too close."

Bruce could not argue with that, not even with his new-found powers of dispute. The truth was that they *were* close. The truth was that if Terrence was going to die, it was going to be very soon. Milton and Bruce could talk about Billyana some other night.

Milton got control over his body, his heart rate, and his

respiration, so he was not acting like an unthinking mammal. He began the final approach to where a flashlight ahead of them was shining, briefly.

The light went off again, and the sounds of movements were clear, two people standing up. Milton could see their vague silhouettes before the lights of the neighborhood below, two people in a hurry, leaving abruptly, the oat weeds whispering around their legs. Terrence—surely that was who it was—adjusted his backpack, slinging the straps over his shoulder, and there was a clink, an aluminum container, maybe a thermos.

Milton walked quickly now, and when he reached the place where they had been he heard a large power spread out from the tree above, a moon-pale ghost extend and slant upward—an immense owl.

Milton went quickly to the crest of the hill. The two figures were not lingering, but were making haste down the trail, appearing and vanishing between the big old oaks, clearly visible, moment by moment, against the background of the pale waterless rye and wild oats.

Milton hurried after them, and Bruce was shadowing his steps, dogging his progress, closing in. With a sudden lunge Bruce reached and seized one of the weapons, and pulled the gun from Milton's pants.

Bruce ran ahead, not bothering to keep quiet now, running fast and noisily, with long strides, the gun held out from his body in his right fist.

Milton could not run so fast.

He tripped over a tree root and went down. He got up at once, but he was out of breath. He wanted to call out, but what would he cry? What words could he use? He wanted to keep his brother from taking a human life, but he was all too aware of the unevenness of their physical abilities, Bruce the athlete and Milton, stubborn and faltering.

A third figure ran up the path from the foothill, a flashlight bobbing and lurching as this new arrival came on fast, appearing and disappearing behind trees.

The third figure joined Terrence and his mother, and a flashlight illuminated the trio. Nina Atwood was the new arrival from down the hill. Milton perceived her pretty face lit up by the flashlight in Terrence's hand. The three exchanged greetings, gathering together.

Before Milton could call out a warning, Bruce was upon them.

46

Bruce's gun arm was extended, his posture stiff, and Milton could see the determination in his aim.

A tongue of flame erupted from the pistol—silent, the flicker of fire making the three figures flinch and crouch, falling away.

Milton was swept with relief as he continued downward along the path, and he was relieved further when he saw Bruce fling the replica gun high, the small flame rising up into the dark, and arcing down into the dry foliage of the hillside.

Bruce turned and hurried up the trail, and at first Milton believed that his brother was motivated by similar relief, and maybe even good humor. But as Bruce got closer Milton grew aware, by the jerky swiftness of Bruce's movements, that his brother was angry.

He was very angry. Milton twisted away from the pathway, just eluding Bruce's grasp.

Milton ran as fast as he could. He crashed through dry

branches and stands of poison oak, moving quickly, thrashing through the undergrowth, with his brother right behind him. Milton was hopeful that he had a certain advantage at dashing and darting, despite his brother's size and power.

But he had not reckoned on his brother's wrath.

Bruce pushed Milton from behind, and Milton stumbled through dehydrated, fallen branches, managing to keep to his feet by a disjointed staggering, running to keep from falling.

"Give me the gun," said Bruce, and this time he struck Milton's back harder, a rib-shaking blow, and Milton's knees buckled.

He tumbled to the ground and Bruce was on him, grabbing and tussling, trying to get his hands on the butt of the pistol. With a twisting, snakelike effort, Milton rolled out from under his brother.

Milton leaped to his feet. He pulled the weapon from his waistband and racked the slide, cocking the firearm and making sure that Bruce heard the sound.

Bruce was undeterred.

He rose and nearly snatched the weapon from Milton's hands. Milton tottered backward, very much afraid of his brother, branches snapping as he staggered down the hill.

Bruce followed, striking Milton's forehead with his fist, a solid, nearly stunning blow that gave Milton an instant, fleeting vision of sharp-edged explosions. But he did not fall, and Milton took heart at this evidence of his own tenacity, and at the same time realized that he could not withstand another similar blow.

Bruce readied another punch, his fist knotted, his feet braced.

Milton shot him.

THE NOISE WAS LOUD and the gun flash bright, an instant of illumination and percussion so vivid that Milton felt his own body go limp, strengthless, beyond any desire to commit further harm.

He had aimed at Bruce's legs, but the decision to use the gun had taken such a brief moment, and the flash of light had been so sudden, that the aftermath was all the more confusing.

Bruce had vanished.

He was nowhere. One shot, and Milton was alone in the parched, fallen, frayed branches of the eucalyptus.

Except that he could hear a small, ongoing, panting noise, like the sound a thirsty animal makes drinking from a pan of water. He located the source of the sound, his brother coiled into a fetal position not far away, but hard to see in the poor light, speechless and gasping.

47

Milton made his consciousness take events in an orderly manner.

He had reached the limit of what planning and care could accomplish. He could not actually see the blood pouring from Bruce's leg in the darkness, but he could feel it on his hand, a pulsing, warm surge, and he could hear the blood spattering on the ground.

He smelled smoke, in addition to the sulfuric whiff of gunpowder. The thrown cigarette lighter had started a fire, and the odor in the night air was the pleasant, spice-flavored tang of weeds and grasses, herbs and thistles, going up in flames. The breeze out of the west made the fire a distant danger for now, but Milton was worried about Mom and the safety of the house.

"You, Milton," said Bruce, barely able to give the words any power, he was shuddering so badly. "You have to get me to a hospital."

Milton bent down to say something reassuring, and Bruce clung to Milton's arm, a grip of numbing force.

"Hurry!" said Bruce.

"A hospital," said Milton, "is definitely one of the possible options."

The problem with a visit to a medical facility, Milton wanted to protest, was that if Bruce showed up at Alta Bates Emergency with a gunshot wound in his leg—through his leg, as far as Milton could determine—questions would be asked. Police would be informed.

"Call an ambulance," gasped Bruce.

"I will," said Milton.

But Milton did not—not right away.

Bruce could die like this, Milton knew.

He could bleed out, or slip into shock, and if that didn't kill him, infection eventually might, over a period of days. Bruce was rolling around, getting dirt and dried bits of leaf in the wound in his lower leg, and Milton was aware that this bleeding Bruce, injured and helpless and possibly dying, had always been one of Milton's alternatives.

Left here alone, Bruce would perhaps not survive the night. And Milton realized the depth of his feeling for his brother, an emotion far greater than any impatience or resentment he ever felt toward this willful, dynamic, annoying sibling.

But nevertheless, people did suffer the loss of a beloved

family member, and they bore up under the sorrow. Milton could console Billyana in the coming weeks and months, and the two of them could share a long, affectionate, and intimate bereavement.

"This," said Milton, "is an important decision, Bruce. If we go to the hospital we are going to jail."

There was slippery fluid all over Bruce's hands, oily and warm. Bruce clung to Milton's arm, but he was not as strong as he had been minutes before. Mom would ask what had happened to Bruce, inevitably, and the explanations would be very hard to fabricate.

"It hurts!" said Bruce.

"A gunshot can't hurt that badly," Milton argued. "You don't even have nerves in the middle of your leg."

"I don't want to die," said Bruce.

Sirens were beginning to stitch their progress through the dark, emergency help already on the way to combat the fire. The flames were far down the hill, undetectable from the stand of trees where Milton and Bruce could hide, if they chose, a long time.

But just then a new flare burst the dry darkness, very close, sparks swirling and circling in the wind, setting the eastern slope alight. A tree not far away crackled, and sound like thunder shook the air, eerie illumination casting vivid shadows.

"They'll ask where we stole the gun," said Milton, speaking loudly over the sound of the blaze. "And then we have to deal with Nina and Mrs. Quinion—and maybe Terrence. The cops might get around to asking where we were this morning, and then—"

His eyes stung—the smoke was fierce. Bruce did not make a response, his eyes bright in the firelight. The heat was fresh and harsh—Milton knew that if he did not drag his brother away now they both would burn alive.

Or maybe Milton could escape, and leave his brother here.

"Please," Bruce gasped.

Here at Milton's feet was a chunk of wood, the thick end of a branch. He picked up the wood with one hand, and dry leaves and twiggy branches rose with the long, far-reaching limb. He could drop this on Bruce's head.

Where was Bruce's newfound power of disagreement now? Billyana should see this, Bruce all but vanquished. He was still breathing—the noise was unmistakable, but pain or loss of fluid, some fluke medical consequence, had taken Bruce down to a small, almost speechless creature. He was conscious—his eyes were open and blinking, looking around, scared and trying not to be more scared.

If Milton crushed Bruce's skull, there would be no kill shot, no evidence of murder. Bruce would soon be a blackened skeleton. Milton ducked as the tree above them began to burn.

But no.

No, he could not kill his brother.

He dropped the scabby, heavy length of tree branch harmlessly to the ground.

Then he hung the pistol by the trigger guard from a bare twig. He felt a distaste for such firearms, unexpectedly, and he suspected the aversion would last a long time.

"Bruce," he said, in a tone of resignation. "You are the least dependable human being I have ever known."

"I'm not either," retorted Bruce, the only words he could get out.

Milton pulled the cell phone from his pocket and called 911.

But he could not speak when the voice asked him the nature of his emergency. He was overcome with feeling, with compassion for his brother and with anguish. No doubt he was shaken by the abrupt noise and immediate impact of the pistol. They really ought to warn people about the dangers of guns. And the fire. He coughed. Who could talk, with all this smoke and noise?

He was surprised that he was so distressed, but there it was—he was upset. He loved Bruce, it turned out, more than he couldn't stand him.

The dispatcher was speaking in his ear.

He said, "My brother has been shot."

48

Milton hauled Bruce to his feet.

This proved to be not much of a struggle—Bruce did not want to burn to death. He pulled his body upward, like someone unpacking a suitcase, arms, shoulders, and last of all the shattered leg. For the limb was surely shattered; Milton could see that now. It was sickening, the way the leg slumped at all the wrong angles inside the pant leg.

Sparks circled downward all around them, and a nearby eucalyptus went off like a huge firework, with a cannon-shot crack and a blinding flare of light.

He wondered if Mom would remember to pull the windows shut so the house wouldn't fill with smoke, and he even went so far as to consider that Mom would have to evacuate the premises, or face burning to death herself.

The potential twin catastrophes—the possible death by fire of his mother, on the same evening that his brother was seriously wounded—gave Milton a sense of thoughtful helplessness. He had felt the same way when Mom woke him and said that Dad had been killed in an explosion. The heartrending event had seemed like something that had happened a long time ago, and was just then being reported.

They scrabbled back to the crest of the hill and over it, back down the way they had come. Bruce was bleeding hard, the fluid pouring down his leg.

"Stay awake, Bruce," urged Milton as his brother slumped heavily against him. Milton had heard of injured individuals who were kept conscious so they wouldn't slip into a coma and die.

Bruce nodded, a heavy up-and-down of his head.

"I'm awake," he said thickly.

They were safer here, but barely. The police, thought Milton, were taking a long time. A helicopter chugged up just underneath the low clouds, sending a ray of light up and down, sideways and straight ahead, but Milton had no respect for helicopters. The airborne contraptions had searched and circled for hours earlier that day, and Milton and Bruce had eluded them with ease.

THE POLICE ARRIVED AT LAST, running through the trees.

There were plenty of cops, and Milton suspected that police from Richmond and El Cerrito had joined the effort. Milton took some pride in this—he admired those bandits and killers who had required tactical squads and special weapons.

The police were armed with shotguns and garbed in flak

jackets, as far as Milton could tell in the bad light, each figure bulky with protective padding, as though Bruce and Milton might be wired with explosives.

Milton was pleased as a beam of light plunged downward through the gleaming eucalyptus leaves, finding Bruce, his leg black with blood.

Police voices ordered them to lie down.

Milton told his brother everything would be all right. He helped his brother to stretch out on the welcoming earth, but then remained upright himself.

To be shot like this, after a long day of accomplishment and disappointment, would be a suitable conclusion, thought Milton.

There are worse things, thought Milton, than being killed.

In the end he recognized the voice of Officer Dean, the normally pleasant officer stepping close to Milton and leveling a pistol right at him. The cop's voice was hoarse, and his face was pale in the poor light, but even now Officer Dean had a trace of his usual good nature.

"Milton," said Officer Dean, breathless but determined, "just do what you are told. We'll take care of your brother."

"What's going to happen to him?" asked Milton.

"Bruce is going to the jail ward at Highland Hospital," was the reply, "and then he'll have a nice long stay at juvenile hall."

But as for me, thought Milton, there would be many

years in a state prison. He knew enough criminal lore to foresee long seasons in Vacaville or Tracy, Lompoc or even Chino, legendary correctional facilities that kept felons safely away from innocent citizens.

The smoke smelled faintly of medicine, curing herbs, and the long-ago wide-awake nights with the windows open, waiting for his dad to come home.

Milton ran.

He was not aware of deciding to run. One moment he was standing there, expecting handcuffs. And in the next instant he was a human jackrabbit, and nothing could stop him.

Officer Dean shouted, and cops came right after him, but Milton did not care if they shot him in the back. He did not care, and this feeling of not caring was like joy.

He tore through a stand of poison oak, knowing that he would suffer a rash and a stew of suffering in coming days because of the toxic leaves, but as he ran he felt his legs grow more powerful and he sensed his body becoming filled with a new source of light. He enjoyed this sensation, like the power of the mind overcoming all physical constraints.

But then he realized that the feeling of enlightenment was not all in his mind—he was on fire. He pulled off the flaming Ben Davis pullover and flung the garment aside. His hair was burning, rivets of hot embers in his scalp. He ran his hands over his head and rolled downhill through the dust and dry leaves, stumbled to his feet, and fell again, tumbling all the way to the sidewalk at the foot of the hill.

He ran north along the road, dodging among the cars parked along Pierce Street.

His burns hurt, but not if he kept running.

49

Nina and her brother took turns with the garden hose, and the firefighters had hoses, too, that ripped the night with hard streams of water. The fire climbed the back fence, and spat and crackled in the coils of the brambles, hissing when the water beat it down. The smoke burned her eyes.

Nina liked the firefighters, men and women in yellow waterproof jackets and helmets with see-through visors. A yellow canvas firehose extended through the darkness, slack and without water pressure, as the firefighters wended the extension through the hulks and silhouettes of Borchard valuables.

When the hose was fully powered, it lashed the dark blackberry vines and ripped the soil, and the first wave of the flames was overwhelmed. The garage roof caught fire, but the firefighters extinguished the embers quickly, blasting them with a fire extinguisher. Louella used an old-fashioned scythe to clear brambles and stalks of fennel, and the firefighters gave her a wide berth to avoid being mowed down themselves.

"Cut down that bush over there," she ordered a firefighter carrying an ax, and he did as he was told.

The wind grew weak and sporadic. Most of the blaze backed up the hill, spilling like a fluid under pressure, and the fire department had easy work then, keeping the neighboring houses safe.

At last, Nina and Carraway sheltered beside the Borchards' house, under an awning near the back porch, avoiding the rain of spent embers. The ash made the fine, metallic sounds of hail as Louella Borchard talked to the police. She had not known anything, she said, about a bank robbery, but she didn't blame her sons for trying to do what they could in difficult times.

If that meant she was an accessory to a crime, she said, then they could put her in cuffs right now. She was afraid of nothing, and if Bruce died in police custody, she said, she would personally see them all sued for damages and mental anguish.

Nina was impressed with the woman's spirit, if not her judgment.

The cops put an evidence tag on the garbage bag of stolen money, but they left the sack in the backyard for the time being, next to the open hole, taking pictures.

Nina returned Carraway's Beretta, and he checked the safety, making sure it was set, before he slipped the pistol back into his holster.

Nina told Carraway about Jerry Palmer's visit, and asked him, point-blank, about the murdered Iraqis. The subject was harsh, almost impossible to talk about, but she had to know.

"Are you seriously asking me," asked Carraway, "if I committed murder?"

"Jerry Palmer said as much."

"How can you even believe that?" he asked. He was offended to the point of incredulity.

"You're different now, after Iraq," she said. "You talk about expendable humans, and robbing armored cars."

"I think out loud," he said. "Thoughts aren't deeds, Nina. I don't murder people."

Nina was close to tears. "Who did?"

Carraway answered, "I know exactly who did."

50

Carraway and Nina made sure that Terrence and his mother were safely in their house, and then the brother and sister walked home near midnight, two exhausted people. Behind them distant fire trucks and cop cars pulsed scarlet, and the sound of their engines was an ongoing presence, the last of the fires nearly out and the police still questioning Mrs. Borchard.

Myrna Hearn had long since stopped watching the fire and gone home, and so had Dr. Cotteral and Hortensia Cervantes, and all the other anxious neighbors. Nina and her brother were alone.

His Prada sneakers were dusty, but for all his weariness, Carraway was bearing up well, perhaps used to being tired. Nina began to see how it might be in a war—you could not give in to fatigue.

She was about to ask about this, when she sensed that they were not alone after all.

A figure stepped out from beside a light-colored PT

Cruiser just as they reached their front lawn. The dim streetlight glittered on the dew-struck blades of grass, and the intruder's shadow was a long, distorted shape on the sidewalk.

"We just need to talk, Carraway," said Jerry, approaching, his hands on his front belt buckle, his stride easy. "Just a conversation, so we can agree on something."

"Agree on what?" asked Carraway.

"What to tell the investigators," said Jerry.

"Why," asked Carraway, "did you lie to my sister?"

"Just because one guy pulls the trigger," said Jerry, "doesn't make him the actual killer, Carraway."

"You know it does," was the response.

"I need your help," said Jerry. "I need you to testify that I was with you all that afternoon. I need you to say that the prisoners ran off, and that you have no idea who killed them."

"I'm not going to lie to protect you, Jerry," said Carraway.

His voice was even, but determined.

"I'll ask you one more time," said Jerry. "Please."

Carraway looked up at the streetlight, and Nina could see how weary he was. But she could also sense how hard it was for him to turn away from an old friend, and how much sorrow he felt when he responded, "No, Jerry. I won't lie under oath."

Jerry seemed to shrink slightly there in the street. He lifted one hand, acknowledging what he had heard. But then he said, "If you don't help me, Carraway, I don't know if I can go on."

Carraway shook his head sorrowfully. "I'm sorry, Jerry."

Jerry walked back to his car, with an odd, stiff-legged gait.

Carraway told Nina, "Let him go."

Of course I'll let him go, she nearly responded. She had no desire to ever hear from Jerry Palmer again.

"What's going to happen to him?" she asked.

"A court-martial and a criminal trial," said Carraway. "I'll be a witness against him. He knows how I feel."

Carraway turned away, and headed up the lawn toward the front door with an air of finality.

But Nina watched as Jerry got into his car. He shut the door, but he did not turn on the headlights.

That long moment, with no engine sound, troubled Nina. The fear that overcame her was a surprise, because more than anything she wanted to be simply thankful that Jerry was about to leave.

Murder demands justice.

The full weight of Jerry's remark earlier that evening fell upon Nina. Jerry's silhouette was a dim presence in the car, and he sat there unmoving. But he was not entirely unmoving.

She approached the pale two-door, and when she stood beside the car she called to him.

There was no answer, and she pattered her hands on the windshield.

"Hey, Jerry," she called.

The interior of the vehicle was dark, and the bedroom lights and porch lights of the houses of the neighborhood reflected off the safety glass. The flashing rhythm and gleam of emergency vehicles at the far end of the street were mirrored, too—a world barely touched by light.

She called again. "Jerry?"

She could not see inside very clearly at first, but then she was almost able to make out what he was engaged in, fiddling with something dark. The object was actually very dark—it was black. He raised the thing to his mouth, holding it in both hands. She knew what it was suddenly, that dark menacing thing—a nine-millimeter automatic, just like her brother's.

She seized the car door handle, and flung the door wide open.

She reached into the car, seizing the gun. There was a loud, percussive crack and a split-second gout of flame from the barrel of the firearm. The interior of the car was instantly filled with the smell of burning—gun smoke and the acrid, singed odor of seared automobile interior. A puncture appeared in the car roof—a bullet hole.

The shot had missed. Jerry was unwounded, and more— he was energized and furious. He thrashed at her, trying to make another, more effective attempt. Nina clung to him as he sat there in the driver's seat, trying to force the gun out of his grasp. She hurt him, elbowing his face, twisting his fingers. But he was strong, and he was hurting her in return, pressing her head against the steering wheel.

Nina did not like that. She dug the point of her elbow hard into his face, and kept hitting him. She hit him more than she absolutely had to, for lying to her about her brother.

CARRAWAY REACHED THE CAR just as Jerry tumbled into the street.

Carraway fell at once to his friend's side, calling his name. Or perhaps he was saying something else—the shot had temporarily deafened Nina. She carried Jerry's gun in both hands, and set it carefully on the lawn.

She let herself down easily, needing to catch her breath. Her elbow was numb, but she could bend it easily. She had struck Jerry with every last bit of energy in her body, and hit him more times than she could count. The dewy grass felt wonderful.

Then Carraway was bending over her, anxiously asking her if she was all right.

Or something like that. She could almost make out the words.

51

Terrence was in his bedroom, safe.

The room seemed larger than usual, and much more quiet.

Even in this secure place he could smell the smoke, the complex scent of eucalyptus, oak, and summer grass.

His mother was on the phone somewhere in the house, her words hard to distinguish, talking to her sister in La Jolla, or her friend in Eureka, her voice rising to excited wonderment, and subsiding to reassurance.

Terrence did not turn on the lights for the moment, but kept the darkness around him. After a long wait, he turned on the lamp beside his bed, and radiance was suffused with shades of gold.

He went over to his computer and used the USB cable to download the evening's recording. He had kept the recorder switched on during their retreat down the hill, and after Nina came to get them, and even as Bruce arrived, breathing hard. Terrence had recorded it all.

He wanted to hear again what Nina had said.

Terrence put on the earphones when the recording was downloaded, and then he had to fast-skip through the waft of owl flight, the muffled racket of the freeway, and the stealthy footsteps of the two brothers.

There it was. Nina's voice.

She stepped in front of Terrence and his mother, shielding them with her body as Bruce panted toward them down the trail. Terrence could hear her now, saying in an even voice, "Put down the gun, Bruce—you're not shooting anyone."

And then there was the click, and another click, again and again, as by a miracle or a chance blunder the weapon did not work. It had not been a weapon at all, as Nina later explained it, but a lighter of some kind, emitting flame but not bullets.

He liked her choice of words. And he loved the way she said it, afraid but not giving into the fear, exactly what Terrence knew real courage was.

Put down the gun, Bruce.

Terrence would cherish this recording.

He played it again.

You're not shooting anyone.

He could listen to Nina forever.